C000016947

MURDER AT MATCH POINT

COURTSIDE CAFE COZY MYSTERIES

MYRTLE MORSE

BRITISH AUTHOR

Please note, this book is written in British English and contains British spellings.

BOOKS IN THE SERIES

HIDDEN TALENT

Everyone exaggerates when they're dating someone new.

It's the same as fluffing your CV before a job interview. If you want to stand out from the competition, a few white lies can make all the difference. They're only there to bridge that awkward gap until the person you're dating has a chance to get to know the real you and unravel the mysteries and idiosyncrasies that make us worth falling for. When that happens, those white lies don't matter anymore. They're something to laugh about while you grow old together and remember a time when you were both strangers trying to impress the other into liking you more.

But not all white lies work out for the best.

And some really come back to bite you at the worst possible time! I thought, ducking to avoid the tennis ball that zoomed over my head with enough speed to knock out a charging hippopotamus.

"Don't duck it! Hit it!" the man on the other side of the net shouted before adding: "With your tennis racket" - as if the most basic concept of tennis was lost on me.

The next ball was a yellow blur when it powered over the white tape of the net.

This time, I executed a martial-arts style manoeuvre I had no idea I knew and succeeded in making contact with the tennis ball. It soared up into the air... over the fence and into the bushes by the side of the tennis court.

Perhaps the shouty man on the other side of the net did need to recap the most basic concept of tennis.

"That'll be one more for Sampras," he muttered cryptically, before shaking his head in my direction. "Racket up. Chopper grip. Step and block. Simple! I've taught two-year-olds who picked this up faster."

I tried not to visibly sulk. Wasn't the person you were paying to help you get better at a sport supposed to be *nice* to you whilst they did it? This felt more like a hazing ritual for an illegal dodgeball club. I would have said something along those lines to the tennis coach - who'd clearly missed his calling as a drill sergeant - but it was my fault that I was in this situation in the first place. And this was the only way out of it.

I gritted my teeth and waited for the next ball.

This time I stepped and blocked, feeling a jolt of elation when the ball hit the strings in the way tennis balls tended to when I saw professionals do the same thing on TV. This wasn't about being best friends with the dictator on the other side of the court with his hopper of balls and smug matching-top-and-bottom-tracksuit. This was about following through...

"Don't follow through!" he barked when I completed the racket swing and the ball dipped straight down into the net.

Oops.

"How about we take a water break?" he suggested after I'd managed to hit about 50% of the next two dozen balls he'd fired over the net. I'd succeeded in nearly hitting him three times and getting the ball back over the net and inside the court only one time fewer than that. In my mind, that constituted a huge improvement, but there was a dazed look in my coach's eyes that hinted I may be giving myself too much credit.

We sat down on the wooden bench, stained dark green in a way that evoked Wimbledon and all things British and tennis. I'd never been one for tennis fever, but now that I was sitting by a court on a warm April day, I thought I understood. It was in the way the birds swooped over the silent courts - empty apart from the two of us - and in the scent of freshly cut grass from the fields that surrounded the Fillyfield courts that whispered of summer picnics and the great British outdoors. Tennis was just... civilised.

I waited until we'd both taken sips of our water before I decided it was time to ask for the verdict. In my heart, I already knew. "How do you think I'm doing?" I tentatively asked, before immediately wishing I could fit into my brand new tennis bag and do the zip up, after seeing the way my tennis coach's facial expressions underwent some sort of seismic activity before he managed to regain control.

He pushed a hand back through the peroxide blonde hair on the top of his head, the highlights a stark contrast with the dark, closely shorn sides where his natural colour showed through. It was not a hairstyle that spoke of maturity, considering that the man sporting the look was in his late twenties, but even though I'd only met him this morning, I got the impression that underneath Oliver Hewitt's carefully curated exterior was a man with a lot more going on beneath the surface than was visible from the first impression.

"The effort level is fantastic," he began, softening the blow.

"But the rest is rubbish," I jumped in, so he didn't have to say it.

Had that been an amused smirk that had passed his lips for a second before disappearing back beneath the 'behave professionally around the new client' veneer he was cultivating right now? I decided it probably had been. I didn't take it personally. I had a strong feeling that a good sense of humour was going to be essential when it came to getting myself out of this sticky situation.

"Can I ask why you've decided to take up tennis? And so, uh... intensely?" he added, trying to word his question as carefully as he could. "Most women just ask me to go out for a drink with them if they want my attention. *Paying* for a whole week of my company is probably overkill." He grinned and looked sideways at me, most likely wondering if he'd taken things too far with that joke.

It was my turn to hide an amused smile and shake my head. I knew how insane this must appear to an outsider.

I had zero prior experience of playing tennis. That had been painfully obvious when I'd stepped out on court today. And for some reason, I'd just booked a one week intensive course that meant we'd be spending five consecutive days together with five hours of training a day. It hadn't been cheap.

To make matters worse, I definitely couldn't afford it.

Things hadn't exactly been going swimmingly in the world of employment. And by not going swimmingly, I meant I'd just lost my job working as a baker for a local cafe which had been forced to close under some very dubious circumstances.

I bit my lip, not wanting to dwell on little problems like being basically broke and without the faintest idea of how I was going to fund any kind of future. I'd already paid for this week's course, and I was going to see it through to the bitter end. After all - wasn't it better to take a risk and hope that it paid off than to never take a chance at all?

I chewed the inside of my mouth, knowing that I was only being so openminded to cover up the fact that I had done something very, very stupid. And all of this was just a desperate attempt to get myself back out of the hole I'd dug myself into.

For the briefest of seconds, I toyed with telling Oliver that I was bored with my fabulously wealthy lifestyle and wanted to get back down to earth and expand my list of fancy hobbies by adding tennis to the list - all so I could go to smug doubles matches dressed inexplicably in knitwear and enjoy barbecues afterwards with married couples whose last names had so many hyphens they were practically unpronounceable. But it was telling a lie like that which had got me into this mess in the first place. In any case, there was something about my tennis coach that made me think he'd see through that excuse in a second.

It was time I swallowed my pride and told the truth about the monumental mess I was in. "I might have told someone that I was really good at tennis when I'm really not," I said, gesturing to the balls strewn across multiple courts at random, in case he needed a visual reminder of just how bad I was.

Oliver rubbed his clean-shaven chin. "And that's what made you decide to learn to play tennis in a week by jumping straight into a routine that's the equivalent of what professional players do when they're training for tournaments?"

He said it as though he just wanted to check he'd understood me correctly, but I knew what he was really asking - and that was for the whole truth. People who tell little white lies about their tennis abilities and then have to prove it at a later date do not suddenly commit to a crazy crash course in tennis. That sort of bad decision was reserved solely for those who'd wildly exaggerated their skill level and suddenly found themselves with an unforeseen amount of pressure to put their money where their mouth was... and a very tight deadline in which to do so.

"I told my boyfriend Chris that I was an ex-junior county tennis champion." At least I'd added the word 'junior' when I'd told that lie. I was still holding on to some hope that Chris could be persuaded to believe that my tennis playing talent had decayed remarkably over time... almost to the point where it appeared to have never existed at all. "The problem is, after I told him that on our first date to impress him - because I knew he liked tennis - he got really excited and entered us into a mixed doubles tournament. Apparently it's quite a big deal." I raised my anxious gaze to meet Oliver's. "Aces on Court Mixed Doubles Championship?"

The way his eyes momentarily widened before being followed by a not so subtle wince told me I was correct about it being a big deal. And even more correct about being completely out of my depth.

He rubbed a hand through his hair, ruffling the blonde strands. "I'm a tennis coach, not a life coach... but have you considered telling him the truth?"

I half-nodded and then shook my head, before wondering how to put the way I felt into words. Prior to Chris, I hadn't exactly had a lot of luck with men. When we'd met over the internet after I'd put up a dating profile in a slightly alcohol-fuelled moment after my job had gone down the toilet, I'd been startled by the connection that we seemed to share on so many things... apart from tennis. Honestly, I'd just got a bit carried away. "I want to give us a chance, and this seems like the only way," was the best I could come up with when I searched for the answer inside myself.

Oliver nodded in a way that made me think it hadn't been such a stupid thing to say after all. "You like him a lot." He tilted his head back and forth, making his blonde hair flip up and down and shine in the sunlight. "Whilst I'm sure you don't need anyone to lecture you that telling the truth from the start would have been a great idea, I do actually admire you for making this commitment. My bank balance does, too," he added with that dark quirk of humour I was starting to see in him. "But... even though we have this week to work on... well, everything," he looked daunted for a second, "... Aces on Court is the most serious amateur tournament in our county. You and your partner will be playing against pairs with years of experience. Decades, in some cases! Even a few local ex-pros enter. I'm not saying we can't make a big difference to your playing in a week, but I happen to know that the tournament is only two weeks away, and when you're starting from zero..."

"I'd need a miracle," I concluded gloomily, having suspected that might be the case from the start.

Oliver pulled a pained expression. "I just don't want to give you false hope. It would take a huge amount of work for a complete beginner to not stick out like a sore thumb in that tournament. You'd have to eat, sleep, and breathe tennis. And even then..." He shook his head and sighed before looking at me with his grey-green eyes. "What sort of skill level does your doubles partner have? He must be pretty good to have been invited to enter this tournament."

Something about the way Oliver took a lot of care to say 'pretty good' implied that 'pretty loaded' was the most important qualifying element.

"I think he's good," I said, having absolutely no idea. Chris had tried to chat to me about tennis, but every time he'd got into anything technical I'd made excuses and dashed off to the loo, knowing the limits of my knowledge would become blindingly obvious if I let things get beyond talking about watching Wimbledon and the Roland-Garros on TV every year. And even that was mostly an excuse to eat strawberries and cream and drink too much Pimm's. "He looked like he knew what he was doing when he mimed some shots?" I added, suddenly inspired.

A strangely thoughtful expression drifted across Oliver's face, like white cotton clouds passing up in the blue distance. "Is his last name Henley, by any chance? Chris Henley?"

I opened my mouth to answer and shut it again whilst I considered what had just happened. "How did you know his last name from my description of miming shots?"

Oliver tried to look apologetic but failed when a fresh grin lit up his face. "Oh, we all know Hands-on Henley here at Fillyfield Tennis Club. He just can't resist. The second he starts talking about something that happened in a match you'd better make sure you're standing a good couple of metres back, because there's about to be a full reenactment for your viewing pleasure."

"Hang on... here at the club? He trains *here*?" As soon as the words left my mouth, I realised that - yet again - I'd failed to think this through thoroughly. When I'd gone on dates with Chris it had been in my hometown of Oakley Down, just ten minutes down the road from the more rural Fillyfield. I should have checked just how many local tennis clubs there were before I'd picked this one - the first result on the internet search I'd run for coaching.

Oliver didn't hide his knowing smirk this time. "You seem to run from one spot of trouble to another," he observed. "Don't worry too much. He's a member here, but he only turns up on Saturday afternoons when the members bring their own bottles and everything gets rather festive and not a lot of actual tennis gets played. That doesn't stop Chris. He doesn't need a court or a racket to play." Oliver pretended to mime a serve and laughed to himself.

I felt like I should probably jump in and defend the man I

was dating, but we were still learning about (and lying to) each other.

A second later, Oliver shook his head and apologised, knowing he'd taken it too far. "So... Aces on Court with Chris Henley. I knew he'd ditched his partner, but I had no idea he'd already recruited a replacement."

Ditched his partner? I immediately wondered, wanting to know more about that story. "Maybe he could find someone else," I said, resigning myself to the truth that a week's worth of coaching was not going to cut it. I'd bitten off more than I could chew this time.

"You're not going to give up that easily, are you?" my coach said, looking sideways at me with an amused sort of surprise tweaking his mouth upwards on one side. "You can handle Aces on Court with Hands-on Henley. I've decided it's my new mission in life. But we should start now. Up! Up!" he instructed, shooing me off the bench.

I wonder what it is about Chris that's caused the sudden change of heart? I thought to myself as I tried to inject some enthusiasm into my already exhausted feet and returned to my side of the net to resume missile practice. But all I said was: "Can you please not call him Hands-on Henley? It's weird." Beyond the world of tennis, it didn't sound like the kind of nickname you'd want to be uttered in public.

No. Wait.

Even *in* the world of tennis, it wasn't great.

Oliver laughed again and shook his head as he lifted his gaze up to those sedate clouds that had no care about the problems of those who stood on the court beneath them. When he looked back across the net, he was serious again. "Now listen carefully, because I'm only going to say this once. The aim of the game in tennis is to hit the ball with your racket." He rubbed his chin for a second as he considered. "Well, it's actually more than that, but... in your case... let's start there."

"I'm not a simpleton!" I sniped back as the first ball crossed the net.

It hit me on the arm and bounced off.

Oh, right... hit the ball with the racket.

When the five hour day came to a close I was bruised and battered both physically and in terms of my pride. But even though I would probably carry the welts from the tennis balls and the blisters on my hands for days to come, I had actually improved.

After we'd taken a short break for lunch, something had clicked in my mind. When we'd reconvened, things had been better. I could now get the ball back over the net with what was starting to be referred to as 'consistency'. I knew my shots were pants and that a passing breeze could blow them off course, but... it was something - which was a lot more than I'd had when I'd arrived in Fillyfield this morning.

A ball rose up in front of me and I hit a forehand that just so happened to connect in the right place. It zipped across the net, landing just in front of the baseline, and I nearly cried tears of joy. Unless I was much mistaken, Oliver was wiping a small amount of sentiment away from his own eyes... or perhaps they were tears of exasperation after the day we'd had.

"That was good," he said, glancing down at the empty hopper of balls before smiling back at me. I'd picked up so many tennis balls today I was certain I'd be seeing them in my sleep. "It was really good. We might actually be able to pull the wool over your boyfriend's eyes," he added, confirming my earlier suspicion that his motive for suddenly saying everything would be fine at the tournament wasn't exactly based on my actual ability and more out of some desire to get one over Chris. I had no idea what Oliver had against him, but right now… I would take all the help I could get, no matter what the murky motivation might be.

I picked up a tennis ball from the back of the court on the opposite side of the net to where I'd been hitting. There were plenty of others keeping it company. "Do you think… do you think tennis might be my hidden talent?" I asked, getting carried away for one crazy second.

I was brought back down to earth when Oliver started to laugh.

He didn't stop laughing for an unreasonably long time.

2

RACKETS AND REBELS

That night and the next, I dreamed of tennis balls.

My new morning routine was watching old videos from tennis tournaments long past and standing in the bath in front of my bathroom mirror swinging my tennis racket, practicing the shape of the shots. That was - until my racket got tangled in the shower curtain. I dramatically slipped on some hair conditioner left in the tub and only saved myself by hanging on to the shower rail… which promptly broke and covered me with plaster from the wall where it had previously been attached.

I was still trying to come up with a plausible story to tell my landlord. I'd accept anything that didn't begin or end with 'I was standing in the bath with my tennis racket'. For now, I'd patched it up as best as I could. I had rent at the end of the month to worry about and didn't need an extra repair bill. My meagre savings were already almost all gone, and when this week of crazy tennis was over, I had no idea what I was going to do.

I'd reached a crossroads in my life that most people would probably one day look back on and say something like: 'And that was the moment I knew I had to set up a business from my bedroom that would go on to become a global super power'. But my memoir would more likely read something along the lines of: 'And that was the moment I knew I finally had to eat the jar of chutney that had been lurking in the back of the fridge for years because there was nothing else to eat'. But I wasn't yet in those dire straits. *I have options,* I tried to tell myself whilst struggling to come up with a single option I actually had available to me. I'd even done the whole 'make a list of your strengths and weaknesses' thing that those chirpy charlatans flogging self-help courses enjoy telling you will solve all of your worries in one fell swoop.

The problem was, I already knew the answer.

I was supposed to be a baker.

Cakes and confectionary had been my first love, and they were likely to be my last - given the way things usually turned out for me when it came to romance.

But I hadn't so much as turned an oven on since the cupcake catastrophe.

I shook my head to clear those thoughts away as I walked along the slightly sandy path that wound down to the Fillyfield tennis courts and my third day of training. *It can wait for another day. You need this time to work things out,* a quiet voice whispered in my head.

The sun was shining again and in the distance I heard the gentle thrum of a lawnmower, sending that scent of cut grass drifting on the breeze again. It would be Easter soon, and that meant hot cross buns and Simnel cake, my baking obsessed brain supplied. I listened to the thought but filed it away... something to consider again later.

My phone buzzed and I glanced down to see a text from Chris asking me how my day was going. My heart jolted sickeningly in my chest. I looked around, suddenly sure he was hiding in the bushes having somehow found out what I was up to. With guilt lancing through me, I hurriedly typed out that I was having a good day and was enjoying the sunny weather. Not a lie in sight. I'd turned over a new leaf. Now all that was left to do was clean up the old ones.

A vision of Chris's blue eyes that crinkled a little in the corners when he looked at me, and his dark hair with its gentle wave that he kept styled to look as though it was just on the imperfect side of perfect swam in front of my eyes for a moment. I felt that familiar warm rush that accompanies the start of new love.

The breeze carried my happy sigh away as I allowed myself a few fleeting moments to think about the man I was dating. Chris was the sort of man that teenagers would plan to be married to by the time they were twenty-one in their bullet-pointed 'life plan'. It would later turn out to be entirely inaccurate when they found themselves perilously close to thirty and regularly having to wear underwear that still had an age label rather than a size because the washing situation had got out of hand again and was in danger of being declared an environmental health hazard. But the reality of adult life compared to a teenage dream probably wasn't something to dwell on.

Chris had his own business that had something to do with trading; he never talked about it in much detail, saying that it was deadly boring. Deep down, I knew he was proud of what he'd accomplished and what success had brought him. He was the sort of person who could actually afford to do crazy things like take a week off for an intensive tennis course, and I had nothing but admiration for him for that. It was easy to think dark thoughts about others' success when you were facing a bump in the road in your own life, but I saw Chris as a beacon of hope.

However, that didn't mean I was completely comfortable with the differences between us. I knew it was pride talking, but I hated to be the one who wasn't in a position of strength. It wasn't about money. It was about having a life to be proud of and having that certainty. It meant you were able to be the best version of yourself. I was a far cry from that right now and edging ever closer to desperation. I knew it was silly, foolish pride, but I hated the thought of needing to rely on anyone apart from myself.

But I didn't have a great track record of keeping my pride under control, did I? That was why I was standing on a tennis court early in the morning waiting for my tennis coach to arrive.

There are worse places in the world to be, that quiet voice whispered in my ear again and I silently agreed with it.

"Good morning! You're new here, aren't you?" a friendly voice said from somewhere behind me.

I turned to see a man in his forties with side-swept blonde hair walk out from the practice court area, hidden behind a screen of trees a little way from the main courts. He was carrying a tennis bag large enough to hold a lifetime's supply of rackets.

"I... I am new here," I confessed, feeling nerves wash over me because of my worry that every social contact brought me one step closer to being discovered by Chris. I'd hoped no one would notice me. With my not particularly flashy ash-blonde hair and average build, I was used to being able to blend into the background when I wanted to. Clothes were always an afterthought and makeup was a special occasion. There was nothing wrong with people who did value those things. It was one form of creative expression. I was just someone who liked to create beautiful things rather than be one.

"Jolly good, jolly good," my new acquaintance responded, striding closer before standing with his hands on his hips and legs spread in a ludicrously wide stance by the side of the court where I'd been about to do some warmup stretches. I suddenly noticed how white - and how very short - his shorts were, before quickly dragging my gaze back up - in case he mistook my alarm for something else.

"Roger Riley, at your service," the short-wearing man announced before springing forward and seizing my hand in both of his. I sidestepped to avoid the huge bag of rackets when it swung round like a pendulum. "Whoops!" he said, roaring with laughter and not relinquishing his grip on my hand. "And you are?"

"Serena," I said, exceedingly reluctant to give him my last name, even though my first was notable enough. All it would take would be for this man to mention meeting me in the wrong company and the jig would be up.

There'd come a time when Chris would inevitably realise I was practicing here, but it needed to be at a stage where I looked like I was putting in the hours for the tournament, not learning how to hold a racket. I was skating on very thin ice.

"It's good to have some NEW BLOOD around here," he told me, shouting half the sentence and nearly giving me a heart attack before carrying on like normal. "We must play some doubles together." His gaze raked up and down my faded jogging bottoms and old comic-book themed t-shirt. To my astonishment, he seemed to see something he liked. "I bet you're a DEVIL on the court, aren't you?"

I feigned a laugh that wouldn't be out of place in an asylum, managing to exhibit enough mirth that I was able to yank my hand back.

"So... how about it?" he asked when I'd realised I couldn't keep laughing in his face forever. He waggled his bushy blonde eyebrows in a suggestive manner that made me wish I *was* a devil on the tennis court - so I could reliably sock him between the eyes with a tennis ball.

"Ooh, I would love to, but I'm not really that competitive?" I suggested before realising that was a rubbish excuse - especially when I was about to undergo another day of intensive training. On the surface, I probably looked like the most competitive amateur player in the world. "When I say I'm not competitive, what I mean is... I can't compete. Legally," I added without thinking it through at all.

Great. Now I sounded like some sort of public danger.

"A devil on the court and a REBEL against the system!" Roger observed, looking more delighted than ever. This was not the reaction I'd been expecting. "I have the solution. How about you and I... one on one, eh? I don't mind a bit of DANGER."

Good grief. He was waggling his eyebrows again.

I was subtly searching for the tennis court's emergency exit when Oliver materialised on the path behind Roger-the-rebel-with-a-questionable-cause.

"Sorry I'm late. I could say it was because of traffic, but I live two minutes away and it's actually because I decided to drink my liquor cabinet last night and I'm horrendously hungover. A word to the wise, ouzo and vermouth do not mix," he announced with all of his usual style and swagger.

I failed to hide my amused smirk. Oliver had managed to keep up the professional facade for the entirety of day one. On day two, something had clicked and he'd figured out we were really doing this for the week. Then the real Oliver had come out. I preferred the real Oliver.

He blinked in the bright sunlight, looking as though he wasn't exaggerating the severity of his hangover. "Oh, you're here, Roger," he said in such a way that left me with no doubt that this man was not his cup of tea. But just in case there *was* any doubt he followed it up with: "Could you *not* be here?"

For a second, Roger's expression went completely blank. I held my breath, expecting some sort of argument to kick off, but the next moment, he threw his head back and laughed loudly enough to make birds take off from their roost in a tree on the edge of the fields around the courts. "Hewitt! You never fail to make me LAUGH!" he finished with a bellow.

Oliver tried to look as though he had been joking, but I caught his eye and was forced to look away to avoid getting the giggles. He'd definitely meant it.

"Much as I've love to shoot the breeze with you two BOUNDERS, I've got a meeting with some of the top blokes in a company whose name I contractually can't speak out loud." Roger mimed zipping up his lips and throwing the zip away, getting his mimes mixed up. "But let's just say... you'd have heard of them."

"No doubt in the papers when they're investigated for fraud every year," Oliver agreed.

The strange blank expression came over Roger's face again before that awful laugh was repeated. I nearly asked Oliver to stop doing what he was doing. The split second before the 'joke' hit home was doing nothing to help my frayed nerves.

"Funny stuff. Funny man." Roger said, miming shooting him with twin pistols. "Catch you all later. Seize the day! Don't do anything I wouldn't do!"

The man was a walking dictionary of clichés... and he didn't appear to know how to use any of them correctly.

"We're doing some tennis training, so I think we've already crossed that line," Oliver remarked.

I was genuinely glad when that snipe blew over Roger's head like a gust of April wind.

"Jolly good. Lovely to meet you, Stephanie," he said, his eyes lingering on me for a moment before that gaze travelled to Oliver and I thought I saw regret that our solo session had been interrupted.

"You too, Ryan," I replied, deliberately getting his name

wrong - whilst being secretly glad he'd clearly already forgotten mine. Thank goodness there were bonafide idiots walking around in the world.

Oliver snorted when Roger looked confused for a second.

The grin bounced back onto the eccentric man's face and he flopped his side-parted head in my direction. "I'll see you... on the court," he finished, swinging round and nearly taking us out with the huge tennis racket bag.

We watched him stride away up the path without seeming to have a care in the world or a jot of awareness of the thoughts of those who watched him leave.

"I feel like I need a shower after that," I said without thinking.

"To get rid of Roger's slimy personality? You're not the only one," Oliver agreed, shaking his dyed blonde hair. "I'm grateful that I have the opportunity to be a club coach here, but it does come with the burden of having to be civil to some complete and utter morons."

I raised an eyebrow at him. "That was civil?"

He grinned. "I make a special exception for Roger. There's just something incredibly annoying about that... NO! Sampras! NO!" he broke off halfway through the sentence, dashing to the side of the tennis court.

3

A MATCH MADE IN HEAVEN

I turned around and was in time to see a huge ginger cat trotting away carrying something in its mouth.

Oliver slowed to a halt and sighed. "That's another one gone."

"You don't approve of cats hunting?" I asked, not sure how anyone could argue against the natural instincts of an animal.

"Hunting?" My tennis coach looked nonplussed for a second. Then he burst out laughing. "Sampras doesn't hunt anything. He's a stray who found his way to the club, probably drawn by the smoked salmon and cream cheese sandwiches that the members bring with them when they come down for afternoon tea socials." He frowned. "In all honesty, surprisingly little actual tennis gets played around here, but I digress. Sampras was fed enough pity treats that he decided to stick around. The club put up 'Cat Found' posters, but I think he'd been on his own for a while. He was a bag of bones when he first arrived. These days... not so much."

I watched as the chunky cat disappeared into the hedgerow that bordered a field. There was no denying he was impressive - glossy and with thick fur that glowed like smouldering embers in the sunshine.

"There was a heated club meeting where half of the members wanted to look after the sweet little kitty cat and the others, who habitually ride across the countryside on horseback terrorising wildlife, had some alternative ideas." A dark expression crossed his face before it lightened again. "Sampras is smart. He knows who to avoid and who's a friend. I actually think the nasty attitudes of some of the members were what made our glorious leader decide that the cat could stay, just to stick it to them. That and I happened to check out his social media at the time and he'd just joined a business marketing group who advocated having an animal around to humanise the business. It makes the extortionate membership fees seem like they come from a human rather than a profit-motivated robot."

"Right," I said, still trying to process how having a cat was a business strategy.

"But all that was before Sampras developed his little quirk. Some people around here argued that it would be useful having a cat around to chase away any field mice who dared to come in search of the crumbs dropped beneath the picnic tables, but Sampras isn't interested in hunting mice. He hunts tennis balls."

I frowned and tilted my head at Oliver to see if he was being serious. Apparently, he was.

"At first, it was funny. Oh, look at the ginger cat carrying a tennis ball in its mouth. Isn't that sweet? But then I started to notice I was losing a lot more balls than usual, and they're not cheap. If I lose even ten balls a week, that's pretty expensive. And worse still, I can't figure out where he's hiding them all!"

I had a sudden vision of a ginger cat sitting in an underground chamber on top of a mountain of tennis balls - like a dragon with its hoard of gold. "Have you tried following him?"

"Of course I have! But he's not stupid. He knows when you're watching and he'll just sit in the hedge until you give up and... and I am an adult man with a tennis coaching business! I will not sink to chasing after a cat who's robbing me blind."

"So, what you're saying is... Sampras is smarter than you," I deduced.

Oliver gave me a scathing look, but I didn't miss the flicker of amusement behind his eyes. "Let's see who the smart one is after today's tennis training."

And that's how Oliver won the argument.

More than five hours later, I was too exhausted to think straight, but along with the exhaustion there was a deep satisfaction in having made visible improvements to my playing. I'd worked hard, and even though he liked to play it cool, I thought that Oliver had secretly been impressed.

We sat on the green bench together as the afternoon sun started to dip in the sky. I was certain that all over England, people were out in their gardens with gin and tonics, enjoying this first flush of spring's transformation into summer. It would be jumper weather in a few hours' time, but that wouldn't dampen the spirits of a country who would don shorts and a t-shirt as soon as the mercury moved into double figures.

"You're doing much better than I thought you would," he said when we'd both caught our breath after the last drill.

I chewed that one over in silence, acknowledging that it wasn't exactly a compliment.

"Have you been practicing at home?" he added, looking curiously at me.

"Oh... just a few shadow shots." I tried not to think about the shower rail.

"I was going to wait until the end of the week to tell you this, but I think you can handle it now." He took a deep breath, alarming me by suddenly going all serious. "I can't in all good conscience send you into a tournament like Aces on Court without you having some competitive practice before you go up against your first opponents. I've arranged a friendly mixed doubles match for Saturday morning. Friendly-ish," he added at the last second.

"A match?" I said, hearing the worry I felt reflected in my voice. I knew it proved that Oliver had a point about not jumping straight into the tournament, but it just felt so soon. I didn't think any amount of shadowed shots in the bathroom mirror would get me ready in time.

"Yes, a match - it's something people who take up tennis usually do so with the goal of one day playing. Because there are *so* many other reasons to play tennis."

"Quit the sarcasm. Who's playing in this match?" I asked, a terrible suspicion suddenly coming over me.

By my side, Oliver squirmed - doing nothing to allay my fears. "You also need to practice with your partner. There's a lot more to tennis than just getting the ball back over the net and in the court. In doubles, there's psychology, a connection between two players, tactics..." He continued to rattle off a list of words, trying to distract me from this great betrayal, but it wasn't long until he ran out of meaningless pseudo-scientific terms and was forced to answer the question - mostly because I gave him a look that warned of his imminent demise if he didn't spit it out.

"Obviously, I've asked Chris to play doubles with you, but..." he quickly added when my mouth started to flap in horror. "I didn't actually mention it's you he's playing with. I just said I had a mystery partner for him to play with in a match against a couple of other club players."

There was something about the way he skated over the

'other club players' that made me move my focus away from the massive mess Oliver had got me into by saying I'd partner with the man I'd lied to about my tennis ability. "Who are the..."

"Louise and Roger. Lovely couple," he added whilst not meeting my gaze.

"Roger as in... the same Roger we bumped into this morning?" I wanted to get this straight.

My tennis coach shuffled his feet. "It was short notice and Roger's always up for a doubles match."

"Because no one wants to play with him," I guessed, pretty darn sure I'd hit on the truth.

Oliver didn't answer, but I took his silence as agreement.

"Look... you're better than you think you are. Maybe you do have a hidden talent after all." His voice went a little too high at the end for him to carry it off believably, and I was long past having any illusions over magically turning into the next Serena Williams. The most we would ever have in common was a name.

I shot him a look that heavily implied he should try again. And quickly.

"You're really not that bad... honestly. I think you can handle club level tennis, if you keep your cool. You've got much better technique than the majority of the players here who've been playing with bad habits their entire life. I've taught you well," he said, unable to resist patting himself on the back. "What they have over you at the moment is experience, which is why it's important for you to play this match. Look on the bright side... if it does go terribly, you won't have to play in the Aces on Court tournament."

"You should have started with that argument," I grumbled, finally seeing that Oliver was right. Better I make a fool of myself when watched by nothing more than the handful of curious cows who lurked close to the hedgerows than by whatever audience there would be at this high-profile amateur tournament. There was nothing to gain by waiting for that day to reveal that I'd not been entirely truthful about my tennis playing past. I liked Chris a lot, but it was almost better that things should go out with a fizzle this Saturday than end with a nuclear detonation that resulted in county-wide humiliation.

"It's the right choice," Oliver agreed, doing some more self-back-patting. "Seriously though, you're starting to look like you know what you're doing on court. I think you might surprise yourself out there on Saturday."

I was still glowing from getting an actual compliment from Oliver when he added: "Plus, I've seen your boyfriend play. He could do with a crash course in tennis himself. What could go wrong?"

With the prospect of my debut in competitive tennis looming on the horizon, the next few days seemed to blur into one. I'd like to be able to say that I made huge strides and felt as though I was ready to take on the challenge, but the truth was, I'd started to take a few steps forward and then a few more back.

After the initial 'how to hit a ball' phase had passed, things had become more difficult. I still thought I was improving, but the more I practiced, the more I saw that tennis wasn't as simple as just swinging a racket at a ball.

And the more I found out about the intricacies of the sport... the more I realised I loved tennis.

But that didn't mean I was totally chilled out for the Saturday morning match. My nerves were so bad, I did something the night before the match that I hadn't done in what felt like forever.

I baked a cake.

What could go wrong? Oliver's voice repeated in my head as I beat the coffee-flavoured buttercream until it grew silky. Visions of me failing to even make contact with a tennis ball, or falling over my own feet, threatened to distract me when I iced the coffee and walnut cake.

I thought I was torturing myself with every worst case scenario possible.

I didn't even come close.

4

CAKE AND CATASTROPHE

Three people were waiting by the entrance gate to the tennis courts when I walked through the car park the next morning. My racket bag was slung crossways across my body and I'd even tied my hair up in a high-ponytail and plaited it - hoping to capture the style of Anna Kournikova if not her on-court ability. I wasn't normally someone who put much stock in the whole 'first impressions count' thing, but today, I was erring on the side of caution. I needed all the help I could get to play the part of a convincing tennis player. I just hoped that my newly purchased tennis skirt wasn't overdoing it.

My grip tightened on the cardboard cakebox I was carrying in front of me. I stopped myself from squeezing any harder and damaging the cake inside.

I'd always turned to baking when I was worried about something. There was a simple sort of quietness that over-came me when I focused on weighing out the sugar and flour and watching carefully when it came to gradually beating eggs into creamed butter and sugar without letting them curdle. It was half-science and half-art and it gave me peace and happiness whenever I opened a recipe book.

Working at a bakery had been great. I'd been able to bake all day without needing to think or worry about anything else in the world. Last night, I'd had to force myself to stop after making the coffee and walnut cake. Otherwise, I'd probably be drowning under an avalanche of chocolate chip cookies and viennese whirls right now. Things had been good when I'd sold my creations for other people to enjoy. It was too bad it had all gone so terribly wrong.

One cake was all I'd allowed myself. One cake was all I hoped I'd need to distract the other players from my performance on the court. A lot could be forgiven and forgotten when there was cake to take your mind off it.

And there was one person in particular waiting by the gate that I wanted to forgive me.

Chris's tanned face broke into a smile when he saw me approach. "That's why Hewitt was so mysterious about who he'd partnered me with." He clapped his hands in a one-man round of applause. "Well played the both of you!"

It took me a second to realise he was talking about Oliver, but using his surname in that annoying way people of a certain class and boarding school background liked to do.

Chris chuckled to himself and shook his handsome head before sticking his hands on his hips and casually glancing across the carpark, allowing me some time to appreciate the strong jawline that would be the envy of many a male model and the classic handsome lines he'd been born with and then emphasised with good diet, exercise, and a slew of supplements I'd seen on his bedside table. It was that attention to health and fitness which had pushed me towards telling the tennis lie. People were drawn to people who understood their way of thinking... their lifestyles... and I'd wanted so badly to be someone who fitted in with Chris's life.

"What am I thinking? Introductions are needed!" he said, ruffling his dark hair, amused by his own forgetfulness. "This is Louise Lovely, and this is Harry Novak. Harry's our umpire for the day," he said, gesturing to each of the other people present in turn. "And this is Serena... someone I am very fond of," he said, not quite going as far as to say we were boyfriend and girlfriend - or even together at all, for that matter.

I smiled brightly at Harry and Louise and stowed that miffed feeling away for thinking about later. "Is there a reason we're waiting here? And I thought Roger was coming?" I added, trying not to sound too hopeful.

"Roger is the reason we're all standing around like lemons," Harry said, rolling his eyes. His face had a hint of sunburn across the nose and cheeks that surely only his exceedingly fair complexion could have caused in the mild British sunshine. "As usual, he likes to keep everyone on his clock."

"Don't be so hard on him," Louise chided, knocking Harry's arm good-naturedly and making her blonde curls bounce up and down where they'd escaped from the ponytail her hair was just a little too short for. "He's probably got a good reason for not being here yet. Did anyone see if his car was in the car park?" Something like uncertainty flickered across her lightly-freckled face when she asked that question, but I couldn't imagine why.

"The car park is huge and people do delight in parking behind trees and bushes for some unfathomable reason," Harry replied. "I do believe that some of us feel that the lack of a gate on the carpark entrance means that the great unwashed will enter and seek out Porsches to vandalise. Don't you own a Porsche, Chris?"

"I do, but it's at home in the garage, not any place where

marauding members of the public could throw eggs at it," Chris replied, his tongue firmly pressed into his cheek.

"What is this, a mothers' meeting?" a new voice interrupted.

We all turned to see Oliver wander out of the car park with his tennis bag slung casually across his shoulders. It pained me to note that out of all of us standing here, Oliver was the only one you would look at and think 'that's a tennis player'.

"I don't want to spoil the knitting club, but are you planning to play tennis at all today?" The tennis coach looked around at us, clearly bemused by the lack of sport taking place at what was supposed to be a tennis club. "Hang on, is that a cake?" His gaze fell on the box I was holding. "What kind is it? I take it all back. Continue with the gossip group if there's cake involved." He reached out and lifted the lid of the box before oohing over the contents. "You're good at baking. Interesting," he finally commented, still eyeing the cake as though he was already devouring it with his gaze.

"It's coffee and walnut, but you'd better wait until you taste it to make judgements like that," I replied with a quietly confident smile. Tennis may not be my hidden talent, but I knew for sure that I could bake my little socks off.

"Unless you iced bathroom sponges and sawdust, I think it's going to be a winner," Oliver said, still focused on the cake. "Speaking of winners... and cake... but mostly tennis..." He rubbed the bridge of his nose, losing focus. I thought I'd probably just discovered his weakness. "Does anyone want to play, or shall we just stand around here all day? Did you bring a knife?" he added a second later. "I don't want to use my hands, but... if there's no other way, then it's a sacrifice I am willing to make."

I shut the lid on the cakebox, silently wishing it had distracted the others as much as it had my tennis coach. To be brutally honest, Louise, Harry, and Chris looked almost pained by the presence of so many calories.

"We're waiting for Roger. He's the one with the key to the court," Louise explained, gesturing towards the padlocked gate.

"Not the only one," Oliver announced, making a key materialise in his hand with a magician-like flourish. He walked over to the gate and moved to insert it in the padlock. "Huh!" he muttered a second later, before turning to show us that the padlock hadn't been locked at all - just pushed back round so it appeared that way.

"Roger's probably messing about on the practice court wondering where we've all got to. He probably wanted to get here early," Harry commented, before glancing over at Louise with something that looked a lot like pity. Once again, I noticed she seemed nervous... as if she hadn't wanted Roger to already be here.

"He should have come and got us," Chris said, shaking his head and forging past Oliver - who was pretending to usher him through the gate before bowing behind his back like a very mocking butler. The others followed.

I threw Oliver a stern look before nodding that he should lead the way.

"I wonder where old Roger's hiding?" Chris called back over the walking group as we trooped our way down towards the courts below. "Hey, Harry... do you remember that time when we found him al fresco with..."

"Not sure I remember that," Harry jumped in, trying to cut him off.

Louise sighed, but she didn't look shocked by the implications being thrown around. Neither was I. My one meeting with Roger had given me all kinds of creepy vibes, and it wasn't often that I was wrong about a first impression. *Unless you count the bakery*, my unhelpful thoughts jumped in before I could clamp down on them.

"Oh look, someone's forgotten their jumper and bags," Chris said as we got closer to the courts.

"I don't think that's a jumper," Harry said when we were a few steps closer and it became clear that the mass lying on the court was not discarded clothing or racket bags.

It was a body.

"Is that blood?" Chris said, grinding to a halt on the path and forcing those behind him to dodge around or fall over like a stack of dominos.

I followed the gazes of my horrified companions and realised that Chris was correct. It looked like someone had spilled strawberry jam all over the dark green court. A person lay face down in the middle of it. The fair hair that wafted up and down in the breeze was the only sign of movement.

The next few moments passed in a blur of thumping hearts and running feet. We rushed down the path and dashed on to the court, only slowing down when we got within a few metres of the man lying facedown.

Roger had arrived early for the match... but so had someone else.

"I can't look," Louise said, turning and sprinting away towards the practice court, her head dropped low and her eyes fixed on the ground.

"I'll check to see if she's okay," Harry muttered. He'd turned pale with a greenish hue that warned he'd probably be just as in need of assistance as Louise if he stuck around here for too long.

"Should we check for a pulse?" Chris suggested, looking mildly alarmed but keeping his expression calm. Only the vein that jumped in his neck showed he was just as shaken as the rest of us.

"I think it's too late for that. We shouldn't touch anything. The police will want everything left just as it is," I replied as a bitter taste entered my mouth. The cake I was carrying in my arms suddenly seemed to weigh several times what it had done before.

"The police. Right, of course," Chris said shaking his head as if to clear it from a particularly heavy fog. "I'll call them at once."

"Roger has definitely seen better days," Oliver commented when Chris had trotted off, looking strangely calm about the whole affair. "And so has that tennis racket. At least he's got plenty more where that came from in his ridiculous racket bag."

Maybe Oliver wasn't as okay as he looked on the surface, or perhaps hiding behind bad humour was his way of coping.

I stepped around and got to see exactly what he was talking about. On the ground next to Roger, just on the other side of his body, was a tennis racket. Or at least - something that *had* been a tennis racket. Now it was little more than a tangled mess of strings and twisted metal.

"Where's the grip?" I wondered out loud, seeing the exposed handle of the racket and realising it looked skinnier than normal.

Oliver rubbed his chin. "Maybe it never had one on it. Could have been a spare racket. He really did have way too many of those. Or maybe someone removed the grip," he added like it was an afterthought before frowning. "You know what? It's probably option B. You'd get some pretty bad blisters if you did that with a racket without a grip." He inclined his head towards Roger's still form. "Shame," he said, leaving me unsure if he was talking about Roger or the ruined tennis racket.

Given the way I'd seen Oliver act around Roger, I was going to assume it was the latter.

"We should probably go and find the others," I said, wanting to be anywhere but standing on a tennis court in the company of a corpse. Worse still, I could smell coffee buttercream drifting up from the cakebox, making a sickening juxtaposition with the scene before us. I was going to end up like Harry and Louise if I wasn't careful. I walked away and placed the cakebox down before sitting on the bench where Oliver and I had spent our breaks the past week.

My tennis coach joined me and we sat in solemn silence for several moments before he cleared his throat and looked sideways at me. "Well... that's one way to win a tennis match."

5

TRUE COLOURS

"I don't believe it." Those were the first words out of Detective Chief Inspector Rosie Pepper's mouth when she walked down the path that led to the tennis courts and saw me standing there.

"This day gets better and better," I muttered when she was still a good distance away and probably couldn't hear furtive mutterings. Oliver shot me a curious look but made no comment.

The gaggle of police officers the DCI had brought with her moved out to secure the scene. Another pulled out a camera and began snapping shots in a macabre photoshoot. The other players returned to join us by the court, drawn back by the sound of the police.

DCI Pepper ignored the scene of the crime and made a beeline for me. "You got away with it last time, but I think it's pretty clear that you are up to your neck in illegal behaviour. I knew you were a bad egg, but killing someone..." She paused to shake her head. "I should have put you away when I had the chance."

I felt my cheeks grow hot and sensed four pairs of

eyeballs fixed on me as the other players, coach, and umpire stared at me like I really was a killer. I would have wrung Rosie Pepper's tanned neck, but that probably wouldn't go a great way towards helping me to clear my name.

"You know that was all a misunderstanding," I managed to squeak out, fully aware that it sounded even more weak and flimsy than when I'd said the same thing after the original incident.

"You didn't pull the wool over my eyes then and you won't do it now," the DCI informed me, taking out an old-school notepad and flipping it open. "So... why did you decide to murder Roger Riley?"

I assumed she'd picked up Roger's name from Chris's phone call when he'd informed the police that there'd been a violent crime.

"I did not murder Roger Riley," I said, stating it extra loudly and extra slowly for the benefit of all the listening ears. "I've only met him once. I'd have no reason to do... something like that to him." I suddenly couldn't bring myself to say the word 'murder'.

"Is that so? I would imagine that in a tennis club of this size members would see each other frequently."

"I'm not a member here. I'm new to the club," I informed her, feeling my stomach twist into knots. Surely she would leave it there? There were others present who were far more likely to be involved with the foul play that had occurred on Court One. People who had known Roger. *And those who'd openly disliked him,* I mentally added, glancing sideways at the tennis coach standing next to me.

"You'll need to verify that. Where was your previous tennis club and why did you move?" DCI Pepper asked, finding a way to pick at everything I said.

"I... I didn't have a club before coming to Fillyfield for some training," I said, doing everything I could to be open and honest. I could feel my cheeks warming again as I sensed things conspiring against me and a secret I'd been so desperate to keep from worming its way to the surface starting to slip out.

"If you aren't a member, then why are you here?"

The pressure was mounting.

"I was being coached by Oliver. We started training this week. I, uh... wanted to brush up on some skills," I said, desperately clawing onto what remained of my credibility on court. I knew it didn't really matter in the face of other things - like being accused of murder - but I could already sense Chris knew things weren't adding up. A line had appeared between his eyebrows, like he was figuring something out.

"Why now?" DCI Pepper pressed, her dark eyes narrowed in suspicion.

I bit my tongue to keep from saying something stupid like 'Oh, I don't know... I thought I'd take up tennis and then murder a man I'd only met once by pulverising him with his own tennis racket' because DCI Pepper would probably take something like that as an actual confession. Perhaps dark humour was my way of dealing with tragedy, too. I felt strangely lightheaded and visions of the last time I'd encountered the DCI kept flashing distractingly before my eyes. "There's an important tournament coming up. I needed to practice for it."

"She's been training all week every day," Oliver jumped in right when I wished he wouldn't.

"Let me get this straight... you go from not being a member of any club or presumably playing at all to suddenly doing a week long course?"

"I needed a crash course, okay? It had been a while." It had been *never*. And by the look on Chris's face, he had just guessed exactly that. *Great.*

I shut my eyes for a second to try to clear away the gut twisting disappointment I felt. I may have just worked for a week for nothing, not even the slim chance to prove myself and get away with it on the court this morning, but there were more important things to worry about - things like proving myself innocent of a crime I had not committed.

"Interesting. You've already changed your story," DCI Pepper observed, seeing the lie and calling me out - which I definitely deserved. "It's almost as if you've lied before. The time when you lied about not being involved in a bakery that was nothing more than a front for a false travel document business springs to mind."

I did my best to keep from sighing out loud. I'd guessed that this was coming. "I *was* involved in a bakery that was a front for a false travel document business," I replied hotly. "BUT," I quickly added when everyone present was looking more convinced than ever that I was a dangerous criminal. Everyone apart from Oliver, who had a look of delight on his face that could only be described as the expression of a person who wishes they had a bucket of popcorn to eat whilst the drama unfolds.

"But..." I repeated, "...I had no idea that the bakery was bogus. I baked the cakes and made the confectionary and the business seemed to be doing really well!" I could feel my cheeks burning again as I came face to face with my own naivety.

With the unwanted gift of clarity that hindsight brings, I was now able to appreciate that it had actually been remarkable just how popular a little bakery situated behind the industrial estate on a street where half the buildings were derelict had been. At the time I'd imagined that, in spite of appearances suggesting otherwise, this was a trendy and diverse corner of Oakley Down. I'd had many fascinating chats with customers about the countries they were from and they'd always seemed so eager to be visiting them again soon. Darren, my manager, had packed their orders in boxes in the kitchen whilst I'd chatted away the days.

It was because I'd been so touched by the many different people who all seemed to be missing their home and seeking comfort through cakes that I'd baked something I suspected would be the biggest regret of my baking career.

"You were baking cakes that were packaged with fake passports in order to disguise what was really going on," DCI Pepper accused. "As if that wasn't enough evidence to lock you up, which it should have been, you thought it was amusing to rub your crimes in the law's face by actually decorating cupcakes with the flags of the countries these people were using illegal documentation to gain access to." She shook her head in disgust.

And there it was… out in the open at last.

The Cupcake Catastrophe.

A reminder of one incident of incredible naivety that had nearly landed me in just as much trouble as Darren - the person who was actually responsible for the whole illegal racket. It was only because he'd done the decent thing and told the authorities that he was responsible for everything, and he'd employed me to cover up the truth, that I was still walking free. He might have also implied that I was a little bit dim in order to get the police to believe it. When faced with the evidence, I wasn't sure that the implication was too far from the truth.

In my more positive moments, I'd looked back and told myself that I'd never seen anything criminal going on because the people I'd served cakes to had seemed like genuinely nice customers with families and friends they'd enthused about sharing their purchases with. Even Darren had seemed like a dream boss - always singing praises to my baking and saying how well the business was going. The thing was, even though the business had been incredibly illegal and potentially unethical, I still wasn't convinced that Darren was a bad guy. I'd always been impressed by the gratitude on the faces of the customers he'd handed the cakeboxes to. Of course, I'd thought it was just because they really loved cake, but it seemed like for some people, he'd been a lifeline to something better.

But that didn't mean I'd totally forgiven him for dragging me into an illegal business and landing me in deepwater with the police. And the way that this murder investigation was heading, I was pretty certain that forgiveness for that was going to take even longer.

"I find it incredibly hard to believe that you're anything you say you are. I bet you bought those cupcakes from the supermarket!" DCI Pepper said, levelling her most heinous accusation at me yet.

"There's no way this is shop bought. It's too good," Oliver called over from where he'd moved back over to the bench whilst the interrogation and destruction of my character had been taking place. He lifted up a slice of coffee and walnut cake for all of us to see.

"Are you eating cake... in the middle of a murder investigation?" DCI Pepper spluttered, momentarily completely distracted from the hardened criminal she'd been questioning (me).

Oliver looked down at the piece of cake in his hand and then back up at the investigating officer. "I think it's pretty clear that the answer to that question is yes."

I'd never have imagined that DCI Pepper could look more infuriated by someone than she did every time she looked at me, but Oliver had surpassed that expectation spectacularly. In two strides she was in front of him, remarkably making a swat at the cake, as if to knock it to the ground.

Oliver spent all day, every day, dodging stray balls fired

from inept students' rackets. He easily avoided DCI Pepper's swiping paw. "I'm pretty sure cake was not the murder weapon," he said, somehow still managing to look like this was all very interesting rather than terrifyingly scary. I was already imagining the interior of a prison cell and wondering if there were any baking opportunities to be found on the inside, or if it really was all lumpy porridge and off-brand baked beans.

"You're acting very calmly about a sudden and violent death. How well did you know Roger Riley?" DCI Pepper enquired, turning up the heat.

Oliver's forehead furrowed as he considered this question as though DCI Pepper had just asked him to explain the purpose of all existence. He used the moment of deep thought to take another bite of cake. "That is good cake," he muttered before swallowing. "Roger and I were great pals. At least... *he* thought we were."

DCI Pepper's expression was that of a dieter looking at a chocolate cake that miraculously contained no calories. "But you weren't friends? You didn't like the deceased?" Her voice morphed into a gentle, reasonable tone as she tried to rein in her delight at the confession she seemed to believe was coming her way.

Oliver shrugged, still looking thoughtful but managing to catch my eye over the shoulder of the DCI. After spending the week with Oliver, I recognised the dark twinkle of amusement that lurked behind his gaze. "Nobody liked Roger. And if they tell you otherwise, they're not telling you the truth."

DCI Pepper goggled at him for several seconds before it finally started to hit home that Oliver was just a strange weirdo and probably not on the cusp of confessing to murder. "I'd advise you to be very careful about what you say," she informed him, clearly not convinced that there wasn't something unhinged about the tennis coach.

Fortunately, the rest of her police team chose that moment to return from their crime scene analysis and DCI Pepper seemed to come back down to earth and proper police protocol. We were divided up and asked to empty our pockets and bags before being patted down. Finally, our statements were taken. I wasn't surprised that DCI Pepper used the time to look over the scene of the crime rather than speaking to the witnesses and potential suspects. She looked like she'd done a full day's work already and it was barely ten o' clock in the morning.

A relatively short amount of time later, we were informed that we were free to go. The tennis courts themselves would remain shut until the police deemed it appropriate to open them again.

Everyone was quiet when we walked back along the path in a group. Oliver and I were at the back of the pack again. I'd been trying to catch Chris's eye ever since we'd both finished giving our statements, but he was doing an excellent job of pretending that I didn't exist. Just as I was about to consider executing an overtaking manoeuvre and running across the grass to cut him off and get him to tell me how disappointed or angry he was with me for not telling the truth about the whole tennis thing - and then persuade him to give me a chance to show him that not only did I now enjoy tennis, I wasn't actually that bad at it - he pulled out his mobile phone and began loudly talking to someone using legal jargon.

"Good idea. We should all call our lawyers," Harry said, taking out his own phone and prompting Louise to do the same. "Geoffrey owes me a favour. He'll see me through this," the umpire muttered - apparently to himself.

"It's a strange way to act innocent, isn't it?" Oliver said from behind me, just loudly enough for me to hear.

I couldn't help but smile, even though the situation was a serious one. He was right. No one had even implied that any of the three people walking in front of us were potential killers, but they were already lawyering up.

Chris turned off his mobile and spun on his heel to face us when we were on the other side of the gate at the top of the courts. "Harry, Louise... wish I could say it was a pleasure. Keep your wits about you." He deliberately glanced back towards the police, who were still swarming over the court. I didn't have to look at Oliver to know he was surely shaking his head at this exhibition of a guilty conscience. Perhaps in the past I'd have agreed with him, but I'd been an innocent person accidentally involved in a crime before, and I could definitely appreciate why caution and lawyers were needed. I was going to have to rely on my wits alone. There was no way I could afford any kind of lawyer.

"Serena... I'll talk to you later," Chris added, not meeting my gaze before spinning back around and marching off across the car park. He hadn't really said anything at all, but I knew my little game was over. I'd done everything I could to make a wrong thing right, and due to events beyond my control, it had all come tumbling down.

Louise and Harry shot me looks that seemed half-pitying and half-accusing before following Chris, probably still thinking about the character commending way that DCI Pepper had called me a criminal in front of everyone present and then accused me of murder. It wasn't a great way to lay the foundations for friendship.

"So... do you want to take the rest of this cake back home with you, or..?" Oliver asked and I suddenly realised I'd forgotten he was still here. I didn't know whether I should be pleased or worried that my tennis coach hadn't run for the hills the way everyone else had after everything that had happened.

I looked back and discovered he was holding the cakebox that he must have managed to scoop up when we'd been dismissed by the police. The cardboard was fairly squashed, and I got the impression it may have travelled under Oliver's tracksuit jacket.

"It's yours," I said, feeling like I never wanted to see another cake again. They'd become a bad luck talisman.

Oliver shifted from foot to foot, making the loose stones on the path crunch as he looked down at the cakebox and then back up at me with the sort of expression that hints something serious is coming.

I braced myself for him to ask me to leave the premises and never, ever return - although, I wasn't sure why I would need to come back. It was over and it had all been for nothing, hadn't it?

"Look…" he said after a long moment of silent thought, "…I know what happened back there was bad, but your boyfriend is out of order to behave like that. Especially when he hasn't seen you in action. We all do stupid things, but it's what you do to fix those mistakes that should matter."

It took me several seconds to realise that he wasn't talking about the murder. He was focused on tennis. "Thank you for the thought, but you were right from the start. It was crazy to think I could cover up a lie by taking a crash course in tennis. I'm sorry for wasting your time with that."

Oliver did some more foot shuffling before suddenly growing still and shooting me a serious look from his grey-green eyes. "I don't like overconfidence in players, which is why I didn't say this before, but I had no doubt at all that you were going to walk onto that court today and Chris would never guess you only picked up a racket a week ago. I'm not sure that I've ever trained anyone with the kind of drive and focus you showed me all this week, and I know you were practicing outside of our sessions."

"Nothing like the threat of total humiliation to motivate you to try hard at physical exercise," I muttered, but inside I felt a small glow of success. I hadn't managed to achieve what I'd hoped I would in this crazy week, but I'd achieved *something*. And even though I was probably not going to be received back here with open arms (nor could I afford the membership fee) I hoped I'd find a way to still play tennis, even if it was up against my garden wall.

"I'll have to remember that tip when I'm coaching the lazy ones," Oliver said, a smirk pulling up his lips. "Do you think you might want to continue having lessons... at a more reasonable pace?"

I looked down at my shoes, wondering how to tell him I'd love to but there was no way I could afford it. This whole venture had been crazy and based on nothing more than pride and a strong need for a distraction, but I needed to pull my socks up and figure a way out of the mess I'd got myself into courtesy of the bogus bakery.

"Busy schedule?" Oliver suggested when I was silent for a long time.

I looked up into his eyes and saw that he already knew. He'd already figured out that I was not a member of the 'life of leisure' club and that this manic week and all the effort I'd put into it was my way of avoiding my real problems. It didn't take a genius to figure it out, given that DCI Pepper had gleefully spilled the beans on my most recent employment history and how it had gone so terribly pear-shaped.

"Not exactly," I said with a sorry smile. "But it was a great week."

"Well... I'll miss our coaching sessions," he told me - probably just to be polite.

I nodded before adding another smile and turning to walk away from the tennis club forever.

"I might have an idea, if you're interested in hearing it," he said when I'd only taken two steps away.

I turned back and discovered he was looking at the cake-box, his forehead lining with thought.

"An idea about what?" I asked, wondering if he was about to offer me a special deal on coaching. Unfortunately, I couldn't realistically even afford to buy the bananas players usually ate during breaks - let alone pay for the time of a coach.

"If you've got a few minutes and don't mind hiking through some bushes with a fellow murder suspect, I'll show you."

"Uh…" I said, not sure how to answer that proposition.

"If it helps, had I been the one to bump off Roger then it would be pretty foolish of me to kill again immediately afterwards and without the helpful presence of any other suspects, because they've all skipped off to call their lawyers." He flipped his free hand palm upwards in a 'how about it?' gesture.

I glanced down towards the police and then back at Oliver. Curiosity got the better of me. "Show me."

6

THE CABIN IN THE WOODS

A smile broke on my tennis coach's face. "Great, let's go." He walked back through the gate before immediately taking a hard right off the path and into some dense shrubbery. Something told me this wasn't going to be a walk in the park.

"What makes you so convinced that *I'm* not the killer and you're the one risking going into the bushes alone with me?" I called after him once we were in the midst of the thicket and the sound of breaking twigs and thorns tearing at clothing filled the air. I hoped the police were too far away to hear the commotion or we'd have even more explaining to do.

"I'm not at all convinced, but I've got to get some excitement into my life somehow!" Oliver replied in his usual tongue-in-cheek manner. I rolled my eyes, safe in the knowledge that I couldn't be seen in the middle of what felt painfully like a holly bush.

"Here we are!" he announced thirty seconds later, encouraging me to push by a particularly prickly yellow gorse. I was starting to resemble a well-used pin cushion.

After saying some words that would shock and surprise my mother, I managed to stumble through and arrived in a sudden clearing. The grass was overgrown here, but there was a path that led off in another direction, following a trail that looked a lot less like a jungle than the route we'd just trekked. I looked at it through narrowed eyes.

"It comes out too close to the courts," Oliver informed me when he saw where I was looking. "That path's been blocked, too. Club members were complaining about the eyesore, so our glorious leader in all his wisdom planted a few evergreens to screen all of this off, instead of doing something constructive. But... this is it," he announced, gesturing towards the building in the middle of the clearing.

Or rather... what might have *once* been classed as a building.

Now, it looked more like an abandoned shed, the dark green paint long since peeled from the wooden veranda and the bricks stained by the moss that had crept its way up the walls. A sign hanging jauntily over the double doors by a single remaining nail read 'Fillyfield Tennis Clubhouse', but it took an awful lot of imagination to imagine the types I'd met at the club spending time at this poky place.

"What happened?" I asked, trying to imagine that there had once been a time when this place had been new and well-maintained.

"It used to be a normal tennis clubhouse. Quite a fancy one, actually. There was a proper bar rather than just a tuck shop, and sometimes you could even order bar snacks and things." He tilted his head wistfully. "It always closed for the winter because it was only here for the members, and they turn tail at the first sign of a chill. One winter, the roof was damaged by a storm and rainwater got in, which basically ruined the interior with damp. It could have been fixed, but the club's owner wanted to ask members to pitch in for the repair cost. There was a big argument and nothing got done in the end."

He shrugged. "That's when the big boss man planted the evergreens, told everyone to forget about the clubhouse, and then raised the membership fees anyway - even though this club has surprisingly poor facilities for the money members are charged. Our infallible leader is running on prestige alone right now. People like to say they're members here. Fillyfield has history. But... reputations can change. You can't just conceal your problems with tall green trees. Come on," he added, walking up to the double doors. The wood creaked ominously beneath his feet when he stepped onto the veranda where a couple of sad-looking outdoor tables, long faded by the weather, still stood - a reminder of summers spent in the sunshine and the glory days of a tennis club.

"Are you sure you're not a psychopathic killer?" I asked, hesitating when I reached the door he was holding open, like a butler welcoming royalty. Or alternatively, like a psycho inviting his next victim into a trap.

"A real nutter would answer no to that question," he replied, not exactly allaying my fears before adding: "Step into the chamber of horrors," which strangely seemed to make things better.

I shot him a look that I hope conveyed how annoyed I would be if he really was guilty and on a killing spree. Then I walked through the doors and wondered if I really was as naive as I thought.

The smell was the first thing I noticed as my eyes struggled to adjust to the dim light coming through windows that were coated with the light green lichen that grows on abandoned places, leaving dust in its wake. It wasn't a foul smell, but it was like stepping into a school changing room where the scent of old sports equipment and clothing mingled with the same pervasive scent of damp that those places always seemed to suffer from. Now that my eyes were adjusting, I was able to see the interior of what must have been the pride of Fillyfield Tennis Club.

It had been beautiful once upon a time.

The bare bones still remained. There was the warm-coloured wood of the bar and an age-spotted mirror mounted on the wall that reflected my own worried expression back at me. A few crusty-looking bottles rested on the counter behind, in-between the cobwebs. The floorboards, while dirty, were hardwood. Beneath the grime, I thought there was still a lustre of polish that whispered of opulence along with the faded wallpaper that had once featured a William Morris design. Over by the entrance to the toilets, sunlight crept in through the hole in the roof which had caused the building to be abandoned as a lost cause.

"I see what you mean about it once being an easy fix," I commented, noting that even now it wasn't a huge hole. Years passing had meant that the floor beneath had rotted away and the building being open to the elements had allowed damp to peel the wallpaper from the walls and cause mould to grow on the cushions strewn along benches. In truth, I thought it all looked a lot worse than it probably was. It certainly seemed extremely petty that the decision had been made to let the once charming place fall into rack and ruin.

"How old is the clubhouse?" I asked, still admiring the craftsmanship of the bar.

"No idea. Maybe close to a hundred-years-old? Stuff was added over the years, but the main part is pretty old. People still come in here occasionally, which would make you think there'd be more lobbying for it to be returned to its former glory." Oliver wandered over to a table up against the wall and indicated a sheet that hung from a nail. "If you want to book a court, you've got to navigate the trees blocking the path and enter this environmental health hazard of a shack. Crazy, isn't it? There's still a lost property box that's probably going to stay lost forever and lockers that will remain unopened and unused."

He walked over to a dust sheet and lifted it to reveal a row of metal boxes up against a wall, the first few spots of rust breaking out from beneath the cream-coloured paint. "It's considered prestigious to have a locker here, even though they're just cheap junk really. Most of them have been passed down through generations." He shook his head. "That's the sort of thing the boss man really needs to consider. History. I'm just a tennis coach, but I'd like to keep my job, and it's in my best interests that Fillyfield doesn't fold. I've heard whisperings of land being purchased nearby by some of our own members and a new club being built - something state of the art and modern that no one really wants. I bet the idea would be dropped in a heartbeat if a few things changed around here." He looked at me like he was expecting me to say something in answer to a question he hadn't asked.

"Well... what do you think?" he added when I stood there like a lemon.

"About what?"

"Taking this place on! Making it a decent clubhouse again and setting up your own cafe. Why did you think I brought you out here, to tell scary stories around a campfire?"

I looked around again at the interior of a building that was a far cry from anything a health and safety inspector would approve of.

"The roof needs repairing," I pointed out. "And the floor beneath."

Oliver nodded. "I'll talk to the big man about it. Just between us, I reckon he's regretting his decision to not act on this sooner. I also happened to find myself in his office behind the tennis courts a few days ago and discovered that membership numbers are down this summer. I think he'll be ready to listen to the idea of an outside business taking over the clubhouse."

"But I'm not a business," I said, already seeing problems with this plan beyond the state of the premises we were standing in. "I'm just me. I don't know anything about running a bakery or a cafe on my own…"

"You mean you managed to work at a bakery without picking up *any* tips on how it's done? In that case, my new best friend DCI Pepper must be wrong about you master-minding an illegal operation. She's overestimated you."

I frowned, unhappy about the way he'd turned that on me. "Even if I could figure out the business side of things… why would the tennis club owner let me do this? I definitely can't afford any kind of rent. What makes you think it would work out?" I was genuinely curious.

Oliver looked down at the cakebox he was still carrying, now adorned with broken leaves and twigs. "I think you've got what it takes. I don't just mean the cake, by the way - even though it is great. During this week, I saw exactly what you can achieve if you put your mind to it. In my book, that's a heck of a lot better than some smug, private catering company, who'd do the bare minimum to make this place profitable and not care about the corners they cut to do it, taking over. Which, by the way… is exactly what the boss man is considering right now. I saw a leaflet on his desk and you actually have to *pay* the caterers to come in and sell food, so I think skipping the rent won't be a problem. I know it's a strange time to be pitching this when there's a body lying on Court One, but…" he suddenly gave me the full focus of his grey-green eyes, "…somehow, I get the feeling it's now or never for you."

I felt a lump form in my throat, made of fear mixed with a

misery that whispered I would never amount to anything and was destined to be a failure all my life.

You could do this. You should try. An unseen voice seemed to whisper encouragement in my ear as I looked around at what had once been and all that could be again when the years had been washed away.

"Do you think you can get enough cash together to get all you need to get started? After the early days are out of the way, all the profits will be yours. And as well as your cakes being delicious, you'll be able to flog all kinds of rubbish to the crowd here, so long as you call it something fancy. These idiots will spend silly money on anything they think makes them look affluent."

I frowned. "I'm not going to sell anything prepackaged!"

Oliver grinned. "See? You're already having ideas for the place. As to what you should call it, may I suggest: 'Oliver's Place' in honour of your founder... me."

"You may suggest it, and it will be duly noted and ignored," I replied with a slanted smile. "I don't know. I might let you down," I confessed, knowing that whilst things would look better after a good clean and patching up, there could be bigger problems lying beneath the surface. Oliver's question about whether I had the cash to get started was a good one. This idea was tempting, but even if the mystery club owner did decide to stump up for the initial repairs and allow me to use the premises free of charge (which was an incredible offer) I knew that if I were being honest, there was no way I could afford it. Not unless I came up with a bright idea.

"You might," Oliver agreed before focusing on me again in one of his sudden moments of seriousness. "But I don't think you will." A grin jumped back onto his face as he thought of something else. "But if it does work out, you owe me free cake for life for being such a great friend. I also might give you some tennis lessons in return, if I feel like I'm eating into your profits." He looked down at the entire cake he'd procured. I sensed this could become a deal that needed renegotiating in the future if he really could put away as much cake as I imagined.

His smile faded back to a more thoughtful expression. "Just think about it," he advised before inclining his head and walking back out of the door, leaving me alone in the abandoned clubhouse with only my thoughts for company.

Or so I'd thought.

A meow suddenly emanated from behind the bar, and a moment later, a large orange cat jumped onto the counter. I glanced back towards the double doors but was forced to conclude there was probably another way to get inside this place... another hole that would doubtless need patching up.

"Hello, Sampras," I addressed the cat who sat and purred, seeming to recognise his name. "Were you waiting for Oliver to leave before coming out?" I asked, remembering what my tennis coach had said about Sampras's kleptomania and his own attempts to uncover the cat's secret stash.

When I approached the bar and stretched out a hand the ginger cat strolled over and pressed his head against my fingers, that purr still whirring like a motor in his throat. I could certainly see how the cat had won the hearts of many of the tennis club's members.

"What do you think about this idea then?" I asked my new furry friend. "Am I crazy for considering it... or would I be crazy to let the chance pass me by?" My gaze roamed the clubhouse's interior once more, trying to imagine it with a future. "It's really not that bad," I muttered at the same moment a chunk of ceiling adjacent to the hole crashed to the floor, making both of us jump.

I blew air out through my mouth and revised my optimistic view that a lick of paint would mean that most of the work was done. Getting Fillyfield Tennis Club's clubhouse back to a state where food could be served was a huge challenge. It was an absolutely bonkers idea for one person to attempt all on their own and without money in their pocket to get it done.

But maybe a bonkers challenge was exactly what I needed.

There was a loud crash as a roof tile joined the chunk of ceiling on the floor.

I tried not to take it as a sign.

7

FORGOTTEN THINGS

There was still crime scene tape around Court One when I arrived at the tennis club early the next morning. The padlock was missing from the gate, presumably taken by the police, and as the birds sang their dawn chorus, I wondered for the hundredth time what I was doing coming back to Fillyfield.

Because you'll never know if you don't try, that unseen voice whispered again, seeming to drift past me on the April breeze. My grip tightened on the bucket of cleaning supplies I'd been able to scrounge from my parents - who'd been only too happy to hear I was finally taking cleaning my house seriously enough to warrant 'borrowing' them. There was nothing quite like a bit of patronising parenting to make you feel ten-years-old again. I could have asked them for a loan to support this crazy cafe idea, but that would have been even worse then begging for cleaning supplies. Instead, I had a business plan written on a few sheets of A4 paper currently stuffed in my back pocket and an appointment with the bank this afternoon to discuss a small business loan. I had no idea how I was going to convince them to lend me the money, but

I was considering bribery by cake in the form of the 'death by chocolate' I'd whipped up early this morning when sleep had deserted me and my fears and worries had sought to claw me down into their murky depths.

Perhaps 'death by chocolate' was not the most appropriate choice of cake in light of recent events, but there was no other cake in the world that I could think of that would do a better job of convincing a banker to hand over the cash. What kind of person hated chocolate? Failing that, I was considering packing a crowbar in the cakebox and robbing the joint. It was always good to have a plan B.

Nobody from the police had been in touch. I took that to mean that they were biding their time and waiting for the results of the post-mortem to come back, in case the cause of death wasn't as obvious as it had appeared. Once the details had been ironed out, I was sure I could look forward to a campaign of harassment courtesy of Rosie Pepper - who seemed convinced that she had a score to settle with me.

Maybe I should bake her a cake and smooth things over, I thought. Knowing my luck, Rosie Pepper was probably one of those deeply disappointing people who preferred savoury to sweet things. And even the best cake in the world couldn't cure someone who'd made a conscious decision to hate your guts.

The blue and white tape made a fluttering sound as the breeze picked up. I turned away from the empty court to face the line of evergreens that had been planted across the path, blocking the way through to the clubhouse. Oliver had called me last night and let me know that he'd been in contact with the club's owner and he'd given his approval for the project and even agreed to foot the bill for the repair job. Even though getting the roof fixed was what would make the real difference, with no job and no more intense tennis practice, I'd decided that today was as good a day as any to begin.

Money worries and murder accusations were not going to put me off.

With the same determination I'd felt to improve my tennis, I squeezed through the trees - hoping that the tennis club owner would also remember to remove these additions, or members were going to arrive for cream teas with sap stains and scratches.

Sampras lay in a spot of sunshine on the veranda. He blinked at me when I walked by but made no move to greet me or stop me. I took it as silent approval.

"Right…" I said, looking at the clubhouse as though I was facing an adversary, ready to do battle armed with rubber gloves and bleach. It was time to roll back the years.

What am I going to call this place? I thought before also wondering if, when this all came together, non-members could visit the cafe. I shook my head and smiled whilst I scrubbed years of grime off the kitchen area. I was definitely getting ahead of myself, but it would be nice to have a business that could function all year round. I'd have to bake a cake bribe for the tennis club owner as well as the bank.

I was on my way to get some fresh air away from the fumes of the industrial strength cleaners my mum had supplied when I saw the necklace. It lay on the table beneath the court booking chart and I couldn't be sure if it had been there yesterday or not. I'd disturbed a lot of things with my frenzied initial approach to cleaning.

I pulled off a rubber glove and lifted up the silver chain, examining the charm that dangled on the end, glinting in the dim light. It looked expensive, and it was obvious that it hadn't been lying around in the clubhouse for too long because the metal wasn't tarnished in the slightest. The star-shaped pendant spun around, revealing an engraving on the back.

"It was on the line," I read out loud. I glanced down at the box of lost property Oliver had mentioned. In amongst mouldy trainers and yellowing sweat-stained t-shirts didn't seem the proper place to leave a necklace. I slipped it into my pocket and resolved to ask Oliver later.

I'd asked him if the police had finished conducting a search of the clubhouse, or if they'd done any kind of search at all in relation to the case, but all he'd said was that they'd told the club owner they'd finished gathering evidence. Barring Court One - which was presumably only taped off so it could be given a thorough deep cleaning - the club was open again.

"Oh!" a surprised voice said from the doorway of the clubhouse.

I looked round from where I'd been sweeping the worst of the debris off the floor. Louise stood in the open doorway, the sunlight streaming in behind her making her curling blonde hair look like a halo.

"I didn't think anyone would be in here," she said, frowning lightly before engaging with what I was doing. "Why are you cleaning this dump? Is this... is this your job now?" There was an unmistakable note of horror in her voice as she contemplated just how awful it would be to work as a cleaner. I decided to ignore it, knowing that picking a fight with a club member was the last thing I should be doing.

Feeling the old bakery routine slipping back into place, I spread a smile across my face. It was never too early to start working on good customer service. "I'm doing what I can to clear the clubhouse before the contractors come to fix the roof. It's going to be reopened soon as a cafe... run by me," I added, figuring it was a good idea to get the word out.

"Nice to hear life is carrying on as normal even though the love of my life was murdered yesterday," Louise replied, her true emotions spilling out in a rush and making me feel awful for momentarily focusing on what I was doing - forgetting that Louise had been in a relationship with Roger.

"I'm so sorry about what happened to Roger. I'm sure everyone at the club is," I tried to compensate, but it was too late and not exactly convincing either.

Louise shook her head, sending her curls flying everywhere. "I know that Roger rubbed people up the wrong way sometimes, but I can't understand why anyone would do that to him. It's just terrible! The police treated me like I was some kind of criminal yesterday because we were in love." A single tear slid down her cheek. She angrily swiped it away. "I know what's going to happen. Someone is going to open their mouth about Roger's problems and then they're going to think I had something to do with what happened, but I could never. I would never! We were working all of that out and he said he was *trying* to be better. I really thought he'd changed."

"What kind of problems do you mean?" I asked as gently as I could. I could already guess what Louise was going to say next, and as for Roger having changed... the vision of our first meeting on Court One swam before my eyes before I banished it.

"Oh, he was fond of female company," Louise said with an angry little shrug, putting it the lightest way she could. "It was something he wanted to change, but it was like a habit... hard to break. I told him I would always be there to help him through it. I forgave him so many times and things were getting better, but you know what people around here are like. They thrive off rumours, and Roger's old reputation is all they'll talk about. People will start whispering nasty things about me and what they think I did to him. But let me ask you this... if Roger was changing his ways, why would I have wanted to hurt him? I was happy!"

I did my best to nod understandingly, privately thinking

that Louise sounded a lot like she was giving me a dress rehearsal of the performance she intended to give when the police came knocking with their questions. Aside from the wilful blindness she was claiming to suffer from when it came to Roger's extra curricular activities - and how she claimed they'd been improving while I was not convinced - Louise was an intelligent lady. And I was not about to underestimate her.

Especially when we were all alone.

"How secure are the courts? There are hedges and fields on most sides. Maybe an outsider could have come in," I said, hoping to show Louise I wasn't accusing her of anything.

"You know what... you're right! It could have been a robbery. People around here know that membership at Fillyfield TC is incredibly exclusive. Plus, you have to be the right sort to get in." She looked me up and down when she said that, leaving me with no doubt that I did not fit whatever these mythical parameters were. "Roger loved expensive things," she said, making it sound like that was a particularly unique quality to have. "Do you know, robbery sounds like the most logical explanation I've heard yet. It's certainly better than the idea that one of *us* had something to do with it."

"Was anyone already at the club when you arrived?" I asked, not as keen to jump on the robbery-gone-wrong bandwagon I'd only invented to calm Louise down a bit. I knew violent crimes did occur, even in quiet villages like Fillyfield, but there was something about the way that Roger had been beaten to death with his own racket and left in the middle of the court that didn't seem like a casual armed robbery. It was a very personal way to murder someone.

"Gosh, let me think... Chris and I sort of arrived at about the same time. Then Harry was a few moments later."

"Did you see any of them drive into the car park, and did

any of them see you?" I asked before regretting being so obvious when Louise gave me a sharp look.

"No. You know the size of the car park. It's basically like driving through the woods until you find a spot to stop. And people do like to park their cars where other people don't normally look," she added, reminding me of a conversation from that fateful morning about making sure the group's precious cars weren't damaged by marauding members of the public.

The sharp look continued as Louise seemed to evaluate me. I was certain that whatever conclusion she'd drawn wasn't particularly favourable. So much for my customer service skills.

"I actually came in here because I've lost something important to me." She marched right by me before peering at the table beneath the court reservation sheets. "I could have sworn..."

"Is this what you're looking for?" I reached into my pocket and held up the necklace.

If I'd been expecting thanks, I was sorely mistaken.

"That. Is. Mine." Louise somehow managed to put a full-stop after every single word, as if she were talking to someone with brains made of custard.

"I saw it on the table and was going to give it to Oliver to find the owner. I didn't think it should be left lying around," I explained as calmly as possible, hoping to avoid an outright accusation I didn't deserve.

Louise just clicked her fingers impatiently, hurrying me to hand it over.

"What does the writing on the back say?" I asked, only too happy to hit her with the same implication she was levelling at me.

Louise's pale cheeks turned rosy for a second when she

realised what I was suggesting. "It says: 'It was on the line'. That necklace was a gift from a friend. Give it back, please."

I obligingly reached out so she could take the necklace from me and found myself moderately impressed when she didn't snatch it.

"Roger... Roger was a good man at heart," Louise suddenly said when a beat of silence had passed. "We even talked about one day getting married, you know... when the time was right. We had our ups and downs and our ons and offs, but he really was serious about us, no matter what some people might try to tell you. I'd never have done anything to hurt him. Although..."

"Although?" I pressed when Louise seemed to lose the will to say whatever it was that had been on the tip of her tongue.

She shook her head. "I probably shouldn't be saying this, but not everyone loved Roger. He did rub people up the wrong way sometimes. Did you know that only a week ago he and Oliver had this huge public fight right in the middle of a tournament? It was so outrageous, there was even talk about banning them both from the club for good. I know a lot of parents cancelled their children's lessons with Oliver because of it."

That explains why Oliver was so eager to agree to the week long course, I thought, silently solving a mystery that had been bothering me from the first day I'd arrived at Fillyfield Tennis Club. I'd figured that Oliver had to be a mediocre coach if he had that much time available, but when he'd been brilliant in his own unorthodox sort of way, I'd been left wondering why he wasn't busier.

"What were they fighting about?"

"No idea, I wasn't there. I did ask Roger afterwards, but he didn't want to talk about it. He said the whole thing was a big misunderstanding and he'd managed to smooth it over with the board of directors - luckily for the tennis coach, otherwise he'd have been out of a job. I'm sure it's nothing to do with what happened, but I think it's important to keep in mind that there were other people who might have had a bone to pick with Roger." Louise nodded as if she were resting her case in a courtroom.

Something told me that all of these speeches may well have been coached. Louise knew she was in pole position for prime suspect - a woman scorned who crept up behind her unfaithful partner and beat him to death with his own tennis racket before cunningly covering her tracks. She clearly wanted to push suspicion away from her, and she was willing to be very ruthless about it indeed.

"I really don't think this is the proper time to be messing around with a cafe," she announced to the room before walking back out of the clubhouse without a goodbye.

"She does have a point," a female voice said when several seconds had elapsed since Louise's flouncy exit.

I took the opportunity whilst my back was still facing the entrance to the clubhouse to pull a very ugly face indeed. I turned to face the new arrival when I'd rearranged my facial features into something more pleasant.

"DCI Pepper, it's..." I trailed off. I'd been going to say it was nice to see her, but that probably wasn't the sort of thing you greeted someone with during a murder investigation, and in any case, it would be a very big and very obvious lie. And I was trying to work on the whole not lying thing. "How can I help you?" I tried instead.

"You can start by explaining what you're doing tampering with a tennis club facility." The notepad came out and was flipped open expectantly.

"I'm cleaning it," I told her, thinking it should be pretty obvious. I'd actually made some decent progress this morning. "Oliver told me that you informed the club owner you'd gathered all the evidence you needed from the club, so it was fine for me to start work in here."

"I thought you were a baker. Or was that just another misunderstanding?" DCI Pepper was on fiery form this morning.

"As you are aware, my previous place of employment ceased trading. This is a serendipitous new project for me. I'm opening a cafe," I told her with my sunniest smile.

"Strange how you claim to have only started coming to this club this past week and now you seem to have landed a lucrative catering opportunity. And someone died in order for you to get it," she finished, making sure that her final accusation coincided with her raising her gaze to meet mine, hoping to see some sort of flicker of guilt.

"I'm struggling to follow your logic. Are you implying that Roger had to go in order for me to be offered the glittering opportunity of setting up a business in a building that should probably be condemned rather than converted? I would love to hear more about that."

"You tell me," DCI Pepper returned.

I didn't try to hide my eye roll. "I'm guessing you haven't found much evidence if you're coming after me with half-baked ideas," I concluded.

I may not have shown any uncertainty, but I saw a flash of annoyance dance across DCI Pepper's face when I said that. The scene of the crime had been a mess, but it must have been a calculated mess if they hadn't immediately been able to collar anyone. Everyone had been swabbed for DNA and given fingerprints voluntarily as well as being searched. Well... everyone apart from me. I'd already undergone the process all too recently when the police had tried to find my fingerprints on documents that would prove my knowledge of the illicit activity at the bogus bakery.

"We're awaiting lab results," the DCI primly informed me.

"A timeline of events needs to be established and questions need to be asked. The culprit for this crime will be found, make no mistake about that. Nobody is getting away with murder."

"Quite right," I agreed, succeeding in throwing her for a second. Whilst it was satisfying to see DCI Pepper lost for words for a few moments, there was something else I wanted to get out in the open. "I know that you're good at your job and you want justice, and that is admirable. I hope you investigate this crime thoroughly and the person responsible is unmasked, but come on, Rosie... can't we both be honest and acknowledge there's history between us that's colouring your opinion? I think it's time we let all of that go."

"I have no idea what you're talking about!" the DCI said, doing some lying of her own when her flaming cheeks hinted otherwise.

I just nodded understandingly, certain that I was right. The old wounds had never healed. "It wasn't me who made that nasty poster about you in secondary school. The reason you found me with a whole stack was because I'd been going around taking them down, not putting them up. I'm really sorry that someone decided to do that to you, but if you really think about it, I think you know deep down who was responsible." I knew the identity of the culprit responsible for the cruel poster campaign from our school days, and I was certain Rosie did, too... she just didn't want to admit that she'd developed feelings for the wrong person and they'd betrayed her trust. Instead, she'd done some early investigation work and claimed she'd caught me red-handed. Only, I'd been in the midst of a humanitarian act, not one of hate.

"That has nothing to do with this," DCI Rosie Pepper replied, furiously glaring down at her notepad. "We are not at school anymore, and I think it's obvious we've all amounted to who we were destined to be."

I let her say it, knowing that this was just her way of coping.

The DCI's dark eyes suddenly looked straight into mine. In them I saw no sign of forgiving and forgetting. If anything, I'd just stirred up the mud that lurked on the bottom of the raging river that divided us. "Once a criminal, always a criminal," she said, pronouncing me guilty.

"Good talk. A lot of bridge building," I muttered, fed up with false politeness when my olive branch had been so totally rejected.

"This is not over," she told me, making her finger draw a circle in the air in front of me before pointing accusingly. "You're going to slip up one day, Serena Perry. Every move you make... I'll be watching you."

"Will you also be watching every breath I take?" I couldn't resist adding.

DCI Pepper shot me a perplexed look before executing a military style half-turn and marching out of the clubhouse - making sure she shoved the double doors open with enough force to shake even more of the faded paint flakes onto the grimy floor.

It was no wonder we never saw eye to eye. She didn't even get my jokes.

8

CHARMING

I was about to return to my cleaning regime and silently fume about all of the pointed fingers I'd already been subjected to this morning when I heard DCI Pepper's voice again.

There was something different about it.

I rushed over to the window and scrubbed away at the glass, clearing it enough that the veranda was visible through the smeary surface.

It took me a few moments to realise what had changed.

She was being *nice*.

"Thank you again for staying behind all day yesterday and explaining to those visiting the club what was going on. It was much appreciated," she said to someone who was currently still hidden from view by a particularly smeary smear.

"It was my pleasure. Just doing my bit to aid the investigation into this terrible crime. All of us here at Fillyfield want this solved as soon as possible. You have my word that the person responsible will never see a tennis court here again."

"Because they'll be inside a prison cell," DCI Pepper agreed.

"I was talking about a lifelong club ban, but there is that, too."

I scrubbed the smear but didn't truly need the visual confirmation I got once it was wiped away. Oliver Hewitt was the mystery man being chatty with DCI Pepper.

"I feel I should apologise again for our heated debate court-side yesterday," he added, sounding more charming than I'd ever heard him sound before.

I narrowed my eyes, bobbing my head up and down as I tried to see if he was being serious or if this was all some dark Oliver-style joke and he was about to say something that would land him in handcuffs in an instant.

"Not at all. You've already explained how your medical condition relating to low blood sugar was the reason for the outburst. The need to medicate with high-sugar cake is understandable. I can see no other logical reason why you'd have wanted to eat it," DCI Pepper added, making me ball up my fists in annoyance. I could put up with people insulting my character but my cakes were a different matter.

"It's very plausible," Oliver agreed, and unless I was much mistaken, he glanced towards the clubhouse when DCI Pepper was distracted by a squirrel jumping between trees and winked at me.

"It was also very kind of you to offer tea and coffee making facilities for those of us who are conducting further investigations at the tennis club today, but I'm afraid I can't accept your offer of using the clubhouse. In all honesty, I don't think any sort of edible *anything* should be produced there ever. You'd be wise to warn your new tenant about that. If I were acting as a responsible member of the public, I would not hesitate to report that place for food safety violations," she informed Oliver, leaning in and smiling - as if they were in on this together.

I pulled a face at the DCI, knowing her attention was too focused on Oliver to notice me. My tennis coach, on the other hand, seemed to possess remarkable peripheral vision. I saw his mouth twitch up immediately afterwards.

"I couldn't agree more. I'll be monitoring the situation very closely indeed," he assured her - like he wasn't just a tennis coach working at the club and had some sort of real power here. I nearly walked outside and called him out for it, but the DCI was lapping it up for a reason I had yet to understand. Yesterday, she'd been willing to slap a pair of cuffs on Oliver and take him away for reckless consumption of a coffee and walnut cake.

What had changed?

"I've been thinking about taking up tennis myself. Know any good coaches?" DCI Pepper said, making me inhale in shock, choke on all the dust I'd stirred up, and then have to dive into the lost property box to muffle the sound of the coughing fit that followed. I was able to confirm that all of the clothing in the box had indeed been worn prior to reaching this final resting place. They'd matured over time to create a hideous miasma I wasn't sure I'd ever be able to forget, or wash out from my hair.

"Are you... using your nose to sort through the lost property?"

I stopped trying to stifle my coughs and turned around with my eyes streaming to see Oliver leaning casually in the doorway of the clubhouse looking as amused as ever. "No... I was..." I trailed off without explaining. It probably wouldn't do any good anyway. "Just assume there was a reasonable explanation."

"Whenever someone faints on court, I come and grab a pair of crusty socks from that box and waft them under their nose. Works every time," he told me as I wiped my streaming eyes, wondering if they'd been caused by the clothing or the coughing. All I knew was that I was very tempted to disinfect my face.

"Since when were you and DCI Prickly-Pepper such good buddies?"

"Do I detect a hint of jealousy?" Oliver joked, his dark brown eyebrows arching upwards as he stepped around the room, observing the work I'd done.

"Yes, actually," I confessed, wishing that my relationship with the DCI was better. Maybe not as weird as what I'd just witnessed whilst spying through the smeary glass, but... better. Better would be less likely to land me in prison for crimes I hadn't committed.

"I'm afraid I can't divulge trade secrets. Not for free, anyway," Oliver said, peering into the kitchen and pulling an impressed face. "Rosie was being a bit hasty saying you should be reported to the authorities. I'd eat a cake that was baked in that kitchen."

I tried not to pull a face at Oliver's casual use of the DCI's first name. "I doubt you'd care where the cake was baked if it's a medical emergency," I said drily.

Oliver's face split into a grin, proving there was nothing at all in the world that could embarrass him. "What can I say? I can be charming when I want to. But only to very special people."

I closed my mouth on the snipe I'd been about to make about him never showing me any sort of charm. He'd already checkmated me.

"Did you come in here for a reason?" I asked, still feeling like this entire venture wasn't really happening yet. At any moment, I was expecting the rug to be pulled and for the tiny window of hope of being able to bake and perhaps not be destitute doing it (if things went well) to be slammed shut in my face.

"Does a coach need a reason to see his student?" he replied and then frowned. "I suppose the answer to that is yes, or it does get a little creepy." A second later, the glint of amusement was back. "I was just wondering when you thought you might want more tennis lessons. If you were serious about carrying on with all of that."

I tried to think back to exactly what we'd said yesterday morning right after we'd been released by the police. There'd been something about a lifetime of free cake, but I wasn't sure how serious he'd been about that. "I wouldn't feel right asking you for more lessons without being able to pay you properly for them."

Oliver nodded, his eyes scanning the bar and the before vs. after look that was going on where I had yet to finish the polishing job. I had a feeling that by the time I was done, it was going to be stunning. If I could persuade people to look at the beautifully oiled bar and ignore just about everything else inside the clubhouse, I'd be onto a winner.

"I did mean what I said about the cake. I figure I'm going to be spending a lot of money in here otherwise. You may even end up regretting our deal. Which is why I'm willing to take an I.O.U." He turned to look at me. "You made great progress this week, but in my experience, staying good and making improvements takes consistent practice. My schedule is changing around a bit at the moment, so how about any time I have a free slot, you could come down to the courts and play? You'll be here anyway, won't you?"

"Unless DCI Pepper manages to find even a shred of evidence she can pin on me."

Oliver smirked. "She seems like a lovely lady to me. I don't know what your problem is."

"And I don't know what you said or did to get her to

change her mind about you... but I've decided I don't want to know."

"I'd offer to put in a good word for you, but she seems so much happier when I do the exact opposite."

"Please stop talking," I said, scrubbing the surface of one of the tables and pretending I was wiping the holier-than-thou expression off DCI Pepper's face.

"So... who do you think topped old Roger? That is, assuming my favourite DCI isn't correct about it almost certainly having something to do with you."

I shook my head and looked heavenwards for a moment before seeing a damp stain on the ceiling and moving my gaze hastily back downwards. I needed to focus on one thing at a time or it was just too depressing. "I had nothing to do with anything. The only time I met Roger was that day on court when you were late."

"You weren't too keen on having him as a doubles opponent," Oliver pointed out.

I glared at him. "There's a big difference between 'not too keen' and taking matters into my own hands with a tennis racket. If I'd wanted to avoid the match, I could have pretended to have come down with a bug. That's a lot easier than the alternative! I saw Louise this morning," I tacked on, realising I had some questions of my own to ask my tennis coach.

Oliver laughed quietly. "And who did she try to pin the crime on to move suspicion away from herself?"

My expression must have said it all.

"Me? Really? I expected better from her," he commented, still sounding amused. "The thing you should know about Louise is that absolutely nothing in the world is her fault. She bounces from one disaster to the next - always playing the tragically stoic heroine who somehow remains chirpy through all of the bad things life throws at her. If you ask me..."

"Yes?" I prompted when Oliver looked like he might be about to swallow his words.

"I think a part of her enjoys being the victim. That's why she and Roger were such bad news together. He liked to stray and she liked to absorb all the pity she could get for it. And now he's dead. It makes you wonder... how much sympathy is something like *that* worth?"

I felt my eyebrows push up high. Those were some pretty dark thoughts from my tennis coach. "She claimed that you had your own bone to pick with Roger. Apparently you had a big bust up at a tournament around a week ago?" I heard the worry reflected back in my voice and I knew that I didn't want Louise to be right. I didn't want Oliver to have had anything to do with this.

"I can't believe I'm the one she picked out of the lineup," he said, shaking his head and looking like he wasn't taking this seriously for a second. "Harry was an equal part of that argument, but he kept his cool - whereas Roger and I were always ready to butt heads. In this instance, it was because I caught the cheating rat at his usual game and called him out over it. That sort of thing was nothing unusual. Everyone knows Roger was a cheat, but this time it was more impor-tant than your average run of the mill match, so I complained. Harry decided he was going to back Roger, like the spineless worm he is, and I complained about that, too. Loudly. And with many accompanying gestures."

"I can imagine."

Oliver shook his head. "The world of club level tennis is packed with fudged scoring and dodgy line calls, but this mattered. It was a qualifying match for a scheme that gives players a chance to get further in their careers... maybe even bring them all the way to Wimbledon, and that ego trip of a man wanted to take that from one of my most talented teenage students by trying to push his own interests forward. He was watching the other end of the court when my guy hit a clear winner and he called it out… as a spectator! It was a crucial point and there was no way it should have been allowed to stand. The umpire hadn't called it, but half-wit Harry decided he'd take Roger's word for it. I'd heard rumours about Roger exerting a certain amount of influence over his friends, but this was just ridiculous. It completely threw off the rest of the match for my guy. He ended up losing to someone who shouldn't have stood a chance against him. I told Roger exactly what I thought about his little bit of skullduggery. And things sort of escalated."

"I see," I said, actually finding that explanation to be quite reasonable, if Oliver's perspective on the matter could be relied upon.

"That's such a cheap shot from Louise. Especially when she knows there's no shortage of people who had their issues with Roger. The police should be looking a little harder in the direction of people who had business dealings with him. You should hear the things whispered about him and Chris on the club grapevine. I've heard many tales about how their joint business ventures might have been less than ethical. Some even say they dealt in secondhand jewellery, if you know what I mean…"

I frowned wondering if he was implying my probably-not-boyfriend was involved in selling stolen jewellery. "Chris is a trader," I said, feeling sure that Oliver had to be mistaken.

"Is that what he tells the ladies? I guess that does sound better than saying you're a wheeler dealer. Both he and Roger were in that line of business. Clearly, they were successful enough to impress the board into letting them into the club. Having said that, I think Chris is a legacy. That does open doors here."

"It could just be jealousy," I countered, not wanting to jump to any dark conclusions.

"It could be," Oliver chirpily agreed, "or they could both be shady crooks and when one business deal went wrong, the other business partner decided it was time to get even. I did actually hear they weren't on the best terms recently. Maybe something happened."

I crossed my arms and gave my tennis coach an unimpressed look. "Chris does not seem like that kind of man."

"Maybe you're not the only one who tried to put forward the best version of yourself."

And just like that, Oliver cut right to the bare bones of my short relationship with Chris. We'd never got beyond the first stages of trying to impress each other, and I had never stopped to consider that he might have been playing the same games I'd been drawn into playing - all in the name of appearing to be more than we really were. There was a life lesson to learn from that about being secure in your own skin, but right now, I was more focused on Chris's hypocrisy after the way he'd acted when my truths had swum to the surface - that was, if what Oliver was saying had a grain of truth to it.

Did I act too hastily? I wondered, suddenly considering how Chris had come into my life at a time when everything had been going wrong, and I'd so badly wanted something to be going right. I tried to think back and analyse what it was I found attractive about Chris beyond his outward appearance. I thought it had been his confidence and that air of success that hung around his shoulders like a rich mantle. *You wanted what he had, not him*, the voice inside me whispered, telling me what I'd probably known deep down all along.

"That doesn't mean it can't work between us," I said out loud, momentarily forgetting Oliver was there.

"That is entirely your choice," Oliver said seriously. "I'm just a tennis coach, but I think trust is pretty important. And when the close business partner of your boyfriend has just been murdered in a very violent manner... I'd say that you'd need to be completely convinced that you could trust him before taking sides. Ask him about his business," he advised before nodding his head and turning to leave. "I'll let you know about the tennis lessons. Keep your racket with you at all times. You never know when you might need it."

And on that slightly alarming note - depending on how you interpreted it - he left me alone in the clubhouse with a slew of murky thoughts for company.

I tried to continue cleaning the tables, but after a few moments of cathartic scrubbing, I found I needed to catch my breath. All of a sudden, dust seemed to be everywhere, in my nose, in my throat... choking and impossible to breathe through. Recognising that this wasn't dust at all but the beginnings of a panic attack, I downed tools and left through the kitchen exit of the clubhouse I'd pried open from the grips of ivy that morning.

The fresh air felt like soothing cotton sheets against my face, clearing the sudden sensation of choking dust and bringing my pulse down. I'd always been one of life's worriers, but recently, things had definitely spiralled downwards. I needed to work out a way to get myself out of this slump and keep a level head, or I could be looking at a serious problem.

I sighed and sat down on the warped threshold of the door, peering out through the woods that continued behind the clubhouse. The distant garden fences of Fillyfield's outermost houses were just visible where there were gaps between shrubs.

"Where do I go from here?" I wondered out loud, everything suddenly seeming like too much to cope with. I'd said yes to this crazy project right after a man had been murdered and the police in charge of investigating the crime really wanted me to be involved in some way. I should probably be working on my defence and filling out any and every job application I could find. Instead, I was here, potentially wasting hours and days with no way of knowing if any of this was possible.

I sighed and bit my tongue hard enough to make my eyes water. When I thought about it like that, it all seemed so hopeless.

A muted meow disturbed the quiet morning air. I looked over to the left to discover that Sampras was on his way out of a rhododendron bush. There was a tennis ball in his mouth, bright and luminous against the light green and brown of the spring woods. For just a second, I wondered if he was going to inadvertently show me where this mythical stash of tennis balls was hidden, but he made a beeline towards me, dropping the tennis ball at my feet and looking up expectantly.

"For me?" I asked the cat wonderingly, lifting up the ball.

Sampras purred in response, swishing his fluffy ginger tail and trotting back to the bush he'd emerged from. The cat disappeared into the greenery, his mission apparently accomplished.

I couldn't help but smile. A cat who thought the world's ills could be cured by tennis balls! I considered the brightly coloured ball and realised that, as crazy as it sounded, it had worked. I was smiling, wasn't I?

And all of a sudden, everything seemed clearer.

I knew things looked bad when they were laid out in black and white, but there was something else inside of me that whispered to keep going and not give up. Now was not the time to walk away. If I did that, I knew I'd forever be asking the question: 'What if?'.

And as far as I was concerned, a life was only well-lived if there were as few 'what ifs' as possible. Worrying wasn't helping. I needed to find some courage and see this through.

Just like cakes need to be put into a hot oven to rise, going through a difficult time could transform you into something bigger and greater than you were before.

"Boy, do I need to bake a cake," I muttered, mostly focusing on the cake part of that analogy.

Some things never changed.

9

LOVE ON LOAN

Two days later, the clubhouse only looked like one hurricane had torn through it rather than ten.

The lustre had returned to the wooden surfaces and a builder had been in to inspect the roof. There'd been a tense few moments where he'd performed the usual routine of sucking air through his teeth and shaking his head before pronouncing it 'not cheap' to fix. Once I'd told him I wasn't the one in charge of approving the repair he'd dropped the act and told me that it would be fine, so long as someone was willing to foot the bill.

Later the same day, Oliver had let me know it was going ahead. From some time this morning, I would have to confine my own work on the building to the kitchen area because the roof and floor were going to be fixed. I knew there'd be a whole new layer of dust and dirt to remove once that was done, but even so, I couldn't help but feel excitement creeping through my bones whenever I paused to look around the building. I was making a difference, and every day, this impossible dream seemed to come a little closer to fruition.

I ran a duster over the table by the wall and accidentally caught the court reservation sheets that hung on a nail. Pieces of satin-finish cardboard went everywhere as the paper tore where the hole punches were punched. I knelt down and gathered up the scattered cards, surprised to see there was writing on most of them. I'd imagined that the sheets behind were empty, ready to be filled by future dates, but it would appear that new sheets were placed on top of the stack and the old dates remained behind, building up on the nail in the wall until it became too much for the nail to take... or someone came along and knocked them down with some over exuberant dusting.

My gaze was drawn to the names scrawled by the courts and I saw several that I recognised. It would appear that the doubles match Oliver had planned for that fateful morning was not an out of the ordinary occurrence. I could see that Louise often played with Roger as her partner. Sometimes Chris's name was there next to hers and Roger played with another female opponent, whose identity seemed to vary week upon week. If Louise imagined that her beau had changed his ways, she was surely delusional - just going by this chart alone.

Louise's no shrinking violet either, I observed, seeing that she was a regular mixed doubles player, often booking courts on weekdays, too. Harry was always in the umpire's seat, but sometimes her name cropped up next to Oliver's - who I could only assume had been drafted in as a paid extra to fill up the ranks. *That might be worth checking,* my brain suggested, making me wonder briefly about the animosity that seemed to exist between my tennis coach and Louise. But the more I got to know Oliver, the more I realised he seemed to have a bone to pick with everyone.

Then there was the weekly singles booking... for Louise and Chris.

I frowned before leafing through other sheets just to confirm. It did appear to be a regular date. At 8pm on a Wednesday night, they always booked Court Three for an hour of tennis. And if the sheets were to be believed, there was noone else playing at the club at that time.

It could just be a friendly match, I reasoned, knowing I had no right to be jealous or even suspicious, given that I hadn't been together with Chris for long. And in any case, Louise had professed how in love and committed she was to Roger. *Unless she lied about that. Maybe she and Roger were two peas in a pod and something got out of hand,* I thought, wondering if there was more between Chris and Louise than just a shared love of tennis.

I shuffled the sheets back together before remembering there was sticky tape in the drawer of the side table - probably left there for this exact reason. Once fixed, I hung the stack back on the wall and decided that I was definitely long overdue a proper conversation with Chris. It was too bad he was avoiding me.

All had been quiet at Fillyfield since my last run in with DCI Pepper. I was starting to think that the police didn't have any idea who'd killed Roger Riley, or why. Whilst I was relieved to not have my old adversary breathing down my neck, it was certainly disconcerting to think that there was still a murderer out there... walking around and acting like a normal person, whilst hiding their darker half.

The soft knock on the door made me jump.

I silently chided myself for letting my thoughts run wild and ceased fighting the cobwebs to see who was requesting permission to enter what I was starting to consider my domain.

Chris was the last person I was expecting to see.

On the morning of the match, he'd told me that he'd talk

to me later. When he'd never reached out, I'd taken it to have been code for him never talking to me again.

"How are you, Serena?" he asked. His voice was friendly, but wariness lurked behind his eyes.

"I'm fine, thank you," I replied, equally unsure about where this conversation was heading. As I stood holding a duster and looking at a man I'd had such high hopes for, I found myself wondering all over again what had been real and what I'd fallen for because of the circumstances. I wondered if there was anything at all left between us.

"I, uh… wondered if you had a moment for a hit about?" Chris suggested out of the blue. "I could probably show you a few things to get you started, if you like," he added.

I felt my teeth grit involuntarily. A week ago, that might have been a fair comment, but I felt a sudden need to prove myself. I'd put the work in to not be bad at tennis… and it would appear that the day of reckoning was here. "Sure. I've got my racket right here," I told him, grabbing the bag I kept behind the counter in case Oliver had some free time.

Chris looked surprised by my acceptance, making me think it had been meant more as a jibe than an invitation. I just kept smiling brightly at him and we left the clubhouse to hit the courts. It was time to find out if those lessons had paid off.

I tried to ignore the way my hands were already slick with sweat when I took my racket out of the bag. What if I couldn't remember how to hit a ball?

"I heard you were messing around in the old clubhouse," Chris said, picking at the strings on his sleek all-black racket. "You should have told me you'd lost your job at the bakery. I might have been able to help. I have a lot of contacts."

Too late I remembered that mentioning my employment status had been yet another thing I'd glossed over when we'd been on dates. I hadn't wanted to be a failure or someone who could be viewed as a burden. Plus, I'd been so certain that something would come up and I'd have a new job in no time at all.

One week of job searching had been all it had taken for me to realise that there were too many bakers in the world and not enough bakeries.

"Contacts to do with your business?" I asked, seeing an opportunity to find out more about the sort of 'trading' Chris was involved in.

"My work brings me into contact with a lot of different people," he said vaguely, before immediately changing the subject back to me. "Why did you pretend to be interested in tennis?" He pulled three balls out of his racket bag and pocketed two of them, holding onto the last.

I opened my mouth and shut it again before deciding that now was the time for complete truth. After all that had happened, it was silly to be anything other than honest. "I thought you might like me more if we had that in common, but it didn't occur to me that you might actually want to bring me in as a doubles partner. When that happened, I didn't want to let you down. I thought I could fix it." *And I may even have gotten away with it, if things had gone differently,* I silently added, thinking of Oliver's words and the way I really had improved a huge amount in a week. I was never going to compete in a grand slam, but I also wasn't the worst club player to ever set foot on a tennis court. My hand suddenly felt steadier on the grip of my racket. "But, I know I shouldn't have made all of that up. I'm sorry."

Chris looked at me in silence for a long moment before something changed in his expression and the warmth returned to his eyes. "I bet you're feeling under a lot of pressure right now. Big changes in life can make the best of us act strangely." He walked around the other side of the net. I mirrored his movements until we were opposite one another in the service boxes with the net dividing us.

Chris was throwing me a lifeline and I was very ready to take it. I nodded in agreement and watched as he hit a ball in my direction. My forehand flew right back at him without so much as a wobble.

"I still can't believe I've been given the opportunity for this place," I said, cautiously starting to hope that things could be normal between us again. The second shot was a backhand. When I returned it faster than he'd hit it to me originally, the topspin keeping it in the box, I felt the last of my nerves evaporate. "It's always been a 'one day' dream of mine to own my own cafe or bakery, but now 'one day' could actually be some day soon."

"If you need a financial backer... I could probably make some funds available. I'd give you a good rate when it came to paying it back," Chris said. He looked lot less pleased that I was returning his shots consistently than I'd imagined.

"Thank you for the offer," I told him, feeling a little bit weird about someone I had started to think of as my boyfriend offering me a loan with an interest rate attached to it. I supposed it was business, but it still felt odd. "I actually managed to get a small business loan from a bank." I felt a small rush of pride when I said those words... pride that was probably helped by Chris being the first one to hit a ball into the net.

It had taken all of the persuasive powers of cake to get it, but I'd been lucky.

The manager in charge of my case had shown a visible weakness for sweet things, evidenced by the chocolate wrappers on his desk and shirt buttons that were under a lot of strain. Once he'd taken two bites of the death by chocolate cake that I'd pressed upon him as evidence that I was good at my job, I'd known he was hooked. He'd even asked for the address of the cafe so he could drop by for more when it was open! I'd made yet another mental note to discuss whether or not the cafe could be open to more than just the club members - especially as they seemed pretty thin on the ground right now.

I was yet to meet the club owner, who Oliver seemed to always be in touch with whilst also spending a lot of time snooping around his office.

"That's great!" Chris replied, although there was something in his voice that hinted he wasn't entirely behind his words. The ball came back over the net a little too hard. I let it pass by me, seeing it bounce just inside the baseline. "Listen... I wanted to ask you about something else."

I suddenly got the impression that whatever he was about to say next was the real reason he was here at the tennis club. My heart inexplicably sank. "Ask away!" I said, hearing my own chirpy voice in my ears, perfectly at odds with the turmoil I felt inside.

Chris didn't feed in another ball. "Have the police been applying any pressure to you over the whole Roger thing? They've been asking me a lot of questions about how well I knew the man. I've told them that we had a few business deals in the past, but that was it. I'm not sure why they seem to be pressing the issue."

"They haven't asked me much," I confessed, surprised to hear that they'd been so curious about Chris. Oliver had told me about the business deals between the pair and had hinted that things had not been plain sailing, but I'd wanted to hear more from Chris himself. Now it would appear that I was about to get the chance.

"What sort of business did you have with each other? I heard you might be in the jewellery trade?" I asked as innocently as possible.

Something that looked a lot like knowledge of exactly

what I was saying flashed across Chris's gaze. "I don't know who told you that, but it's not correct. I'm a trader, usually working as a middleman for high end products," he explained, summing up his life's work in a handy elevator pitch that probably came out at all the conferences. "Roger had his fingers in a lot of pies. He traded, too, but usually got to have his hands on whatever it was he was selling. I don't actually ever see the products. I might have invested in a few opportunities he pushed my way, but like I've been telling the police, that doesn't mean we were joined at the waist."

"Were you on good terms?" I asked, wondering if the police had heard the same whispers I had.

He looked at me like I'd asked the exact question he didn't want to answer. "Business is business. You can have professional disagreements that have no bearing on your social life. That's the way the world works. If you get stung trading, you just don't work with that person again."

That sounded a lot to me as though there was some truth to the rumour of a business deal going wrong... which meant there *had* been bad blood between them - no matter what Chris might want to claim about business being separate from personal. Only a psychopath would be able to separate the two completely. My skepticism must have shown on my face because Chris looked annoyed.

"The police seem to think there's something I'm not telling them, too, but I'd hoped for more from you. I'm giving you this chance, even after recent events. Can't you do the same for me?" He took a few steps closer until he was touching the net between us. My heart beat a little faster in my chest the same way it had when we'd first met and I'd realised his profile photos hadn't done him justice. "After all... a woman who will take a crash course in tennis just so that you have something in common is either completely crazy, or someone you shouldn't let walk out of your life so easily," he told me.

I felt my breath catch and a small smile pulled at my lips, even though doubt still swirled inside. Was he saying he thought there might be hope for us?

"You know, you're actually pretty good..." He rubbed his chin before waving the idea away. "Forget I said anything. We should play properly."

My heart jumped as I guessed what his next words would have been. He'd been going to bring up Aces on Court this coming weekend. "Then let's play!" I said, feeling a genuine smile spread across my face.

"We can't be here too long because I didn't reserve this impromptu session on the court sheet. You won't believe how many of the old dears around here will make it sound like you committed a capital offence if you forget to write down that you're on Court Three between two and three and they've decided to invite all of their knitting club down to wage war with tennis balls." He rolled his eyes before a new idea lit up his gaze. "I'd be happy to get some tennis lessons for you. There's a coach here who really knows what he's doing. He's coached professionals and all sorts. If he could give you a few good sessions this week, I bet he'd be able to tell you if you're any good or not. Better to find that out before you invest too much time, right?"

"I think I'd enjoy tennis even if people didn't think I was good," I replied, baffled by Chris's words. Who said you had to be technically brilliant at something to enjoy it? There were plenty of people who couldn't bake a cake to save their life, but they still tried. And if they had fun doing it, then I thought they should keep baking. Not everything needed to be about the end result.

"Right... in any case, Callum's got much more experience than Oliver. That's why Oliver gets given the kids and

Callum takes on those with more experience. Well - that and Oliver can pick a fight with just about anyone over the age of ten. He's got quite a colourful history." He sniggered at what was apparently some sort of in-joke.

It hadn't escaped my attention that Oliver did have something of a short fuse, but I also knew that most of the fights he picked were usually done whilst he was laughing on the other side of his face. I had a shrewd idea that it was how he kept himself amused.

Chris twisted the silver rings he wore on three of his fingers - a little quirk of character that I liked in amongst his slick, successful, entrepreneur-conforming dress sense. Even his no-brand visible tracksuit was definitely the expensive variety rather than the supermarket no-name kind. "I should have let you explain more about what happened the other day when things went so wrong. Nobody's perfect," he finished with what I assumed was supposed to be a comforting shrug. "Maybe some tennis lessons would make it up to you. I shouldn't have been so quick to judge."

"Thank you for the kind offer, but I've done well with Oliver so far and we've reached an agreement already," I said, immediately regretting it when Chris clearly assumed I meant an arrangement that involved something other than a lifetime's supply of cake. "It's not what..." I started to explain, but with truly horrible timing, someone walked out from the practice court area and ground to a halt so suddenly that the loose stones on the path made a loud crunching sound.

"Oh. I didn't expect to see you around here, Chris," Louise said, looking none too pleased to be sharing breathing space with a man she had been sharing court space with on a regular basis.

"I was just about to go," Chris announced, suddenly walking over to the side of the court and shoving his racket inside his bag. He gave me one final unreadable look before walking off the court and up the path, giving Louise a wide berth.

Perhaps the days of weekly matches are over, I silently thought, thinking that I hadn't actually seen anything listed for this week on the charts, or even the week before.

Louise and I looked at each other for a long awkward moment when Chris was gone.

"We were sort of seeing each other for a while," she said, breaking the silence in the worst way.

COURTS AND CONFRONTATIONS

"**I** see," I replied, having guessed something along those lines after seeing the matches and the way the pair had just acted around each other.

"It was nothing official and it ended a few weeks ago, so he hasn't been two-timing you or anything like that. Trust me, I know when a man is that sort. Chris is fairly honourable as they go. We were never going to last, and it was hardly serious. I was too hung up on Roger for that. Part of me thinks the only reason we got together was because we both wanted to get one over Roger at the time. It was revenge," she said in a wistful way that made me think there probably had been a little more to it than that. I was also pretty certain that Chris was the one who'd ended whatever relationship they'd had together. Louise didn't seem completely over it.

"He wasn't happy with seeing me on the side. Said it wasn't right doing that to his friend." She shrugged, still trying to convince me that none of this bothered her.

"I see," I said, not knowing why Louise had decided to confide in me. Chris's past relationships were not actually my concern, so long as they didn't stick around to haunt him... like Louise seemed to be shaping up to do.

The other woman nodded her blonde head, dumping her racket case by the court and pulling out a racket and some balls. "It's tough sometimes. Everyone wants to be my friend, but I don't actually have many friends." She spun her racket in her hands in exasperation. "Women have never liked me and men just pretend to like me until they either get what they want, or I tell them they can't have what they want and then it turns out they didn't like me after all. I only have a few people I can rely on, like Harry and Chris. But it turns out..." She sighed. "Chris is just like the rest of them. I shouldn't have been so naive. I even thought that Oliver..." She trailed off before finishing that tantalising sentence, much to my annoyance. Had Oliver been involved with Louise at some point? He hadn't spoken particularly favourably about her, but I'd seen his name on the match sheets, too.

Louise walked around the other side of the net and hit a ball at me. Hard. "I envied Roger, you know. Not because of the other women, but because he was good at making friends who had his back. He, Harry, and Chris were all so close to one another. They were like the three musketeers - getting successful together and telling each other everything. I wish I had that sometimes."

I wasn't quite in time to bring up my racket and the ball glanced off my forehead. Apparently this wasn't a friendly game.

"They also used to gang up on anyone outside of their little club! I can't tell you the number of times I've been stung by a bad line call courtesy of Harry." She shook her head, but there was a smile on her lips. I didn't fail to notice that she'd made no attempt to apologise for hitting me with a tennis ball. "It's all part of club tennis, I suppose. Whether something is in or out is a topic for debate."

"Do you know anything about a bad business deal between Roger and Chris?" I asked, seizing on the previous mention of the pair and managing a decent sliced backhand return to Louise's next shot.

A crease appeared between her eyebrows. "Even the best of friends disagree sometimes." She smacked the ball back and this time I ducked, knowing it was going way beyond the baseline. The wild shot hadn't stopped me from seeing the disconcertion in her eyes.

It hadn't been a small misunderstanding. And there was something Louise knew that she wasn't telling me.

Something about Chris.

"Let's play some points," she announced, walking over to the side of the court and seizing the hopper full of balls that a coach had left behind. I caught the balls she hit to me, feeling like I was loading up on ammunition for the battle to come.

Louise served first and I realised that I really did have a way to go in tennis if this was the kind of power that was possible. My brain was still admiring the speed of the ball when my racket made contact and all of the muscle memory of a week's intensive training took over. The forehand swept back over the net down the line and I was as surprised as anyone when the ball didn't come back. Admittedly, I'd been aiming crosscourt, but my opponent did not need to know that.

As the tiebreaker progressed, I found myself thinking about tennis and one tournament in particular. When we reached a point where we were due to swap ends, I knew I had to say something. I closed my eyes for a second before a sense of calm overtook me. It was futile to feel bitter, and what would that help anyway? It was better to be the positive force rather than the negative.

I took a deep breath and put aside my pride as we walked towards the net. "There's a tournament on Sunday, Aces on Court. Chris entered a mixed doubles pair."

Louise's face suddenly filled with a disappointment that confirmed what I'd already guessed. She'd been the partner Chris had ditched, and I was the new recruit.

"I'm sure by now you've heard I'm not the most experienced player at the club," I said, putting forward my entry for the understatement of the year awards. "And even though I think Chris is still considering it as a possibility, I've decided that I'm not the person who should be competing in such an important event. You were Chris's first choice. I think you should be the one to play with him."

I suddenly felt the warm glow of doing the right thing that I hadn't felt in a long time. All through this messy debacle I'd let my own pride trip me up. When the truth had come out, it had seemed like I was on my way to redemption, but I knew that until I admitted I had no place at that tournament after only two weeks of playing tennis, I hadn't learned my lesson.

"He'll never agree to it," Louise replied, taking a ball out of her pocket and bouncing it on the floor whilst looking in the direction of where Chris had walked away to be somewhere that wasn't here.

I twisted my racket as I considered. "I think he will," I finally decided. "You've known Chris for longer than I have, but he strikes me as someone who likes to win. And he has a much better chance of that with you than with me." I mentally patted myself on the back for being such a good sport.

"That's true," Louise happily agreed, making me regret it immediately. "Maybe he's still around. I'll go find him and talk. Who knows what might happen? You don't know unless you give it a try!" She sounded incredibly chirpy for someone who'd just lost the person they claimed was the love of their life. It was made worse by the fact that she was talking about a man I was currently in some sort of relationship with. Admittedly, I wasn't quite sure where we stood on that, and I was even less sure about my own feelings.

"You don't mind clearing the court, do you? I'd better see if I can catch Chris." And without waiting for my response (which would have been that I *did* mind actually, and she could jolly well send him a text) she grabbed her bag and skipped off up the path like a cheerful lamb.

I turned and looked behind me at the tennis balls at the back of the court. Then, I gazed at those on the other side. The number seemed to be pretty even and there were fewer balls resting in the net on my side. The score had remained fairly neck and neck.

"Not bad. Not bad at all," I said with a smile, feeling that small victory warm me from head to toe. Oliver had told me before the day of the fateful match that I was better than I knew, but it had taken today for me to prove it to myself. *Sure, there are areas where I can improve,* I thought, rubbing the spot on my forehead where the ball had hit and wondering if I was going to have a comedy-style bump there, but I wasn't the worst tennis player in the world. And things could only get better.

I looked around to see if Oliver was lurking, but the courts seemed to be deserted apart from the low thrum of machinery that told me the builders had just started work in the clubhouse. I tried not to think too much about the way it sounded like they were taking a chainsaw to the building and hoped that there would be some structure left when they were finished.

It will be fine, I silently reassured myself. *One more deep clean, and you'll be practically ready to open!* That thought made the seeds of hope I'd been nurturing inside my heart burst into bloom as the reality of what I was doing really hit home.

I was going to open my own cafe... and it was going to be a brilliant adventure.

I laughed out loud, safe in the knowledge that no one was around to hear me.

Which just went to show what a bad idea it is to ever assume something like that.

"I knew it. I knew you were cracked," DCI Pepper said, materialising like a bad dream from around the side of some rickety storage sheds close to the practice court - where everyone seemed to lurk these days. "Maybe that's what I've been missing. If the killer is crazy, then of course that's why nothing would make sense. That's it. It has to be!" Her eyes widened and a smile spread over her face. "I'll see you on the other side of some bars!" And with that final promise, she dashed up the path, genuinely looking as though she'd solved a mystery that had driven her round the bend.

I tried to piece together what she'd just said but ended up conceding that if anyone sounded crazy, it was her. DCI Pepper had made up her mind about me back when we were at school. Now she seemed determined to make the crime fit the person she'd already labelled as a criminal... by trying to arrest me for murder.

My small victory on the tennis court suddenly didn't seem so important when facing the prospect of a lifetime in prison.

Even worse, I'd definitely developed a bump on my forehead.

THE PRANKSTER

It was lucky that the criminal justice system did not rely on things like 'gut feelings'. Otherwise, two days later, I would not have been free to walk down the sandy path that led to Fillyfield Tennis Club and breathe air that seemed heavy with the promise of rain.

I looked up at the darkening sky and wondered whether I had enough time to practice a few serves to sharpen my mind before making my way to the clubhouse. The roof had been fixed in the nick of time. The blue skies that had whispered so tantalisingly of summer had been snatched away in a cruel reminder that summer was not a sure thing in England. It was no wonder that whenever it was sunny we all liked to fling ourselves outside like sun-dried tomatoes. Many even ended up with more than a passing resemblance to tomatoes by the time the day was over.

I opened the gate and walked onto Court One, glancing at the spot where Roger had spent his final moments.

"We're never going to forget that, are we?" someone said.

I looked up in surprise and discovered Harry was sitting

in the umpire's chair with his head in his hands, gazing at the same spot.

"Probably not," I agreed, privately thinking that we were wired that way as human beings. Seeing what had happened to Roger brought home the fragile balance between life and death in a way that felt like a sucker punch to the gut. Of course our brains were reluctant to forget.

"He wasn't as bad as people like to say," Harry informed me.

I nodded, wondering why everyone seemed to want to give Roger a eulogy along those lines.

"Were you close to Roger?" I asked, saying something to fill the awkward silence that had fallen between us.

Harry rubbed his chin and nodded. "I'd known him for years along with Chris. As time goes by, even the closest of friendships can drift apart, but... mostly, we were as thick as thieves." He smiled a little sadly. "I'm supposed to be umpiring a match this morning, if you're wondering why I'm here. I didn't check the weather forecast before coming out and they've just cancelled but... I just wanted some time to remember Roger."

I nodded understandingly. Everyone had their own way of dealing with grief. "I heard that there was an incident at a tournament here a short while ago. A line call was made by Roger and you decided to uphold it, even though you hadn't called it out?"

Harry's thoughtful expression vanished in an instant, replaced by one of annoyance. "I see you've been chatting to Oliver. Let me guess... did he also imply that Roger was blackmailing me in order to fix something as unimportant as a junior tennis match?" He sighed. "Honestly, that man can make monumental mountains of trouble out of the most paltry of molehills. I don't know where he gets these conspiracies from."

I tried not to show surprise at the word 'blackmail' cropping up. Oliver had implied that Roger held influence over his friends, but he hadn't gone that far. "So... Roger definitely wasn't blackmailing you?" I asked, watching Harry's reaction rather than listening to the actual words he was saying. His pulse was visible in his neck, and I sensed that I was not hearing the full truth.

"Of course he wasn't! Look, Roger was the kind of person who was always ready to seize the advantage. Sometimes, he didn't always stop to consider the other person's feelings in the matter, but it was never serious..."

I raised my eyebrows. This sounded an awful lot like Harry confessing that Roger had been blackmailing him.

"It was just one line call!" Harry protested, seeing my expression. "He may even have been right about it. I just agreed more readily than normal because... because he was talking about submitting this ridiculous photo he'd taken of me to the annual tennis club calendar. I figured that if I did him a favour, he'd reconsider. It wasn't blackmail at all. It was just my own silly need to not look like a fool."

He glanced at me and sighed, knowing what I was going to ask next. "I sat on a jam sandwich someone had left on the umpire's chair and it absolutely ruined my white shorts. As soon as I realised what had happened, I jumped down from the chair and was looking at this ghastly raspberry jam stain on my white shorts when Roger snapped a picture. He said that it was going to be 'Mr January', which was utterly ridiculous. I tried reasoning with him, but he was typically Roger about it... enjoying teasing me. I know it was wrong to listen to him over that call, but I just got it into my head that it would be a gesture of good faith which would mean he'd let the blasted photo thing go."

"Did it work?" I asked, curious as to how much of a manipulator Roger had really been.

"I'm not actually sure if that was what did the trick. I chatted to him the day before..." he gestured to the place on the court, "...and he said he had a much better photo of Chris he was going to send in. Apparently, he caught him at the exact moment he wasn't paying attention at the net and the face he's pulling right as the ball is about to sock him on the nose is very amusing. You only get to send in one photo for this calendar to make it fair to everyone, so that was that. It really wasn't a big deal."

He frowned. "Just between us, I think Roger might have used that photo to get back at Chris after he found out he'd been spending a lot of time around Louise. They were supposed to be on one of their many breaks, but Roger mentioned he was going to ask her to marry him soon, so I doubt that he meant for Louise to be having that much fun on her own. And with his best friend!"

He cleared his throat and suddenly looked like he regretted saying so much. "But back to the point... Oliver is right that I shouldn't have taken Roger's word on that call. I am sorry about that. We all knew that Roger's eyes were a bit blurry when it came to deciding if the ball was out or in."

He meant Roger had been a dirty cheater.

"So... you were back to being buddies again?" I asked, not sure if I was convinced by this strange tale.

"As much as anyone ever was with Roger. He did have his moments, you know... moments of brilliance. And his sense of humour was something else. Too bad it was often at the expense of others. Let's just say... that sandwich didn't get on my chair by itself," Harry told me, smiling wistfully as he thought of old times spent together, never to be recaptured. "He didn't deserve what happened to him. I'm just afraid that..." He trailed off and looked at me like he was about to tell me Christmas had been cancelled.

I knew exactly what that look meant. "You think Chris might have had something to do with it?"

"I wouldn't like to say something like that." Harry looked seriously conflicted. "It's terrible to hope for, but I've got everything crossed that this was done by someone who saw an opportunity to make some money stealing something valuable off poor old Roger. I think the police are starting to lean that way themselves."

When they're not leaning in my direction, I thought darkly. "Was anything actually stolen from Roger?"

Harry rubbed his chin. "No idea. Roger liked flashy things, but..." His mouth curved up into a rueful smile. "Let's just say they were branded products sold by alternative producers. I mean, they were good enough to fool all kinds of people, so perhaps the thieves were taken in. The police ask their questions, but they don't like to share anything in return. I've told them the same thing I told you. They seemed equally interested in the idea of blackmail being a motive." Harry managed a smile and shook his head. "Roger was a dear friend of mine, but I do hope this comes to an end one way or another - even if the answer is not one any of us wants to hear." He cleared his throat. "Especially when certain evidence was removed from the scene."

"The grip on the racket?" That had been a hot gossip topic all week at the tennis club. I'd heard all kinds of outlandish theories about where it could have gone during the time I'd been fixing up the clubhouse. Members had drifted in and out to book courts and I'd heard every word of their conversations.

"People are saying that it was taken because of fingerprints... but I asked DCI Pepper about that and she actually gave me a straight answer. She doesn't think the surface of a grip would yield any viable fingerprints. It's not the right sort of surface. You'd be more likely to get a good match from the racket frame, apparently, but that was wiped clean. It makes me wonder if there was something else on that grip. Something that would give the game away." He shook his head. "I don't know what that could be, but it makes you think, doesn't it?"

He slapped both thighs with his hands, making me jump off of the train of thought his words had pushed me to embark on. "Right!" he said - which was British-speak for 'I should be getting going'. He climbed down the steps of the raised up chair as the first few drops of rain fell from the sky, splashing onto the court and releasing that rainy day smell that carried memories of summer downpours and picnic panic, where shelter was hurriedly sought beneath trees.

I didn't wait for Harry to get around to saying goodbye. Instead, I gathered my racket and tube of balls that were not going to get hit today and raced the rain, running up the path and dashing between the evergreens, seeking shelter in the place that was already becoming a second home to me.

The clubhouse roof no longer leaked.

Standing inside a building that such a short time ago could accurately be described as a shack, it felt like the biggest sign that everything was going to come together. The area where the builder had rebuilt the roof was not particularly pretty, nor were the mismatched new floorboards beneath, but a lick of paint and a pot of wood stain would fix that, and then... *It will be time to find out if this business has legs,* I thought, solemnly remembering the money I owed to the bank and what would happen if I didn't succeed.

I shook my head to clear away the worries. I had to throw myself into this wholeheartedly and work the hardest I'd ever worked in my life. If I did all of that and still failed, then I'd have no regrets.

"This is your one big chance," I reminded myself aloud. Rain drummed down on the newly repaired roof and the clean windows showed ribbons of silver falling from the sky and bouncing off the dark green leaves, before dropping onto the pine needled floor outside. All around was a scent of pine needles and wet wood that made me think of summers spent in a wooden cabin in the South of France.

"You're definitely mad," someone said from a dark corner of the room.

I turned and discovered I wasn't nearly as alone as I'd thought... and I really did need to stop talking to myself in front of DCI Pepper.

"Are you sheltering from the rain, too?" I asked her, not feeling any of the usual temptation to start an argument and prove that I was innocent of all charges. Maybe it was the soothing sound of the storm, but I didn't feel that pouring venom on an open wound actually helped anything.

"I suppose I am," the DCI replied, but not nearly as snappily as usual. Perhaps the weather was having a similar effect on her, but when I walked over to the table she'd chosen tucked away in the corner, I thought something seemed different. My old nemesis had always been buoyed by her enthusiasm and driven by tenacity, but today the characteristics I actually admired about Rosie Pepper were absent. Instead, she seemed distracted. An ancient sugar packet had been opened and spilled across the table for her to draw meaningless geometry in, like an alchemist doomed to write calculations forever and never discover the secret of turning lead into gold.

Against my better judgement, I sat down opposite on a rather fancy hardwood chair I'd cleaned and polished a day ago. I tried to find the perfect question to ask - one that wouldn't trigger whatever it was in DCI Pepper that found me so unbearably annoying - but I drew a complete blank. In the end, I reached out and took a sugar packet of my own to fiddle with, watching as the granules spilled across the table from the faded paper packaging.

"I suppose you'll have to clean this up," DCI Pepper said without emotion.

"There's always something to clean up, but if you had the time to make the mess, there is also the time to clean it up," I said, sharing one of my mother's most nonsensical proverbs. She was wasted in the 21st Century. Ancient philosophers would have loved her.

It was surely a sign that all was not well with DCI Pepper because she nodded rather than scoffing. "I hope the mess I'm in will be cleared up soon," she revealed, rubbing her chin and looking across at the rain streaked windows. "Everyone and their wife has lawyers around here, and n one seems to know why someone would have wanted to murder Roger Riley. Having said that, no one actually liked him that much either - apart from that ridiculous hanger-on, Louise." She made a sound of disapproval. "But nothing seems to have *changed*. In my experience, people resort to violent crime when something changes and they feel like they have no other choice. It triggers something that leads to a snap decision. It's not a gradual buildup of annoying behaviours that one day pushes someone over the brink. Murder is so often an act of desperation." DCI Pepper sounded like she'd swallowed a textbook on the topic which, given her academic record, she probably had.

"You can't find anything that Roger had done recently that might have sparked this?" I queried, trying not to think too hard about the things I knew of - like the argument over the line call with Oliver, and the business deal going wrong with Chris. I still sensed I didn't know the full story about that.

"I've heard about some recent incidents, but in all honesty, none of it seemed to be breaking the habit of a lifetime. The only notable change around here has been you." DCI Pepper's eyes suddenly seemed to regain focus, zeroing in and making me wonder if all of this had been an act to lull me into a false sense of security before she began her usual accusations.

She looked away again. "But even that lacks evidence. The entire case lacks evidence. I'm being asked to answer for the absence of progress and there are no shortage of people who want to tear me down, let me tell you." She laughed bitterly. "I guess I climbed over a few people in order to get to where I am in my career without thinking too hard about it. Now they're waiting in the wings to do the same to me."

"Sometimes the obvious thing that's been right under our noses all along isn't obvious until much later when the punchline is revealed," I said, unable to help myself from pushing her to see the parallels between her current lack of vision on this case and my own shortsightedness when I'd been working at the bogus bakery. "Not everything goes the way we plan," I added.

She nodded her head, still gazing at the windows in the opposite wall. "Exactly! I thought I was going to leave school and do something that mattered and helped other people. I believed that if I joined the police and then worked my way up through the ranks, taking every fast-track scheme I could and working myself to the bone, I'd achieve it all that much quicker and be able to help people and use my intelligence for good, but..." She sighed. "...I suppose that hasn't exactly gone to plan. Not every case can be solved the way they make you believe on TV. It might sound hard to believe, but sometimes I'm not even sure if I'm the good guy. Things are not as black and white as the law makes it all sound."

"You don't say?" I said, trying to hold in the sarcasm.

DCI Pepper nodded, fortunately taking me seriously. "All I ever wanted in life was to be able to do the right thing... do the good thing, and now... I don't know. I've done all of this and I still feel like no one actually likes me." Her eyes suddenly filled with pain. Some inner mechanism must have shouted at her that this was too much and reminded her of who she was talking to because her vision unclouded in a second.

"I'm sure that's not true," I said, still hung up on how to offer consolation for someone who definitely hadn't done a lot to make me like her. She'd always seemed like a robot whose sole purpose in life was bringing about my destruction until this strange meeting in the clubhouse.

"That's just the sort of naivety I'd expect from someone like you... or at least, that's what I'm *supposed* to believe. You play the character of Little Miss Nice, but I know you're hiding something. A leopard never changes its spots, and there's more running through your veins than sugar, spice, and all things nice."

With a single swipe of her hand, she pushed the remnants of the sugar onto the floor, scattering the granules across the wood like the wind casts sand across the plains of the earth.

"I'll find the evidence I need, and if all of this comes back to you..." Her dark eyes met my grey gaze. "...I wouldn't be surprised in the slightest." She slid sideways and stood up from the wall seat, casting me one final look of deep mistrust tinged with what I knew was regret over speaking so frankly a few moments before. The DCI stalked across the room and opened the double doors, only hesitating for a millisecond before deciding that torrential rain made better company than I did.

I looked down at the sugar patterns I'd drawn on my side of the table. A sky of crystallised stars gazed back at me reminding me that there was always hope to be found if we will just open our eyes and look for it - even in the most unexpected of places. Somehow, I didn't think DCI Pepper knew how to look for signs the same way I did.

But that didn't mean I couldn't harbour hope for her... and today, she'd shown me more of her true self than I thought she'd shown anyone in a long time.

FIRST BAKE NERVES

The first cake was a disaster.

When I took the tin out of the oven and looked at what could only be described as a biscuit, rather than a Victoria sponge, I told myself it was just first bake nerves. That and I'd never been able to bake a successful Victoria sponge cake in my life - which made me wonder what I'd been thinking when I'd picked that cake to test the clubhouse's old, but seemingly functional, oven.

The internet had recommended a simple Victoria sponge as a good way to test an oven, but it had neglected to say that things would go better if you could actually whip one up successfully in the first place. I wasn't shy of saying I had a talent for baking, but everyone has something that eludes them - no matter how much you follow recipes to a tee and investigate the science of why that darned cake won't rise. After all that had been done by me time and time again, I'd come to accept that there had to be a little dash of magic possessed by smug Victoria-sponge-succeeders that I lacked.

"Lemon drizzles are better anyway," I muttered, slinging the unintentional biscuit into the bin and resolving to start with something different. My favourite was a variety that made use of polenta, and was gluten-free, but not in the usual dry-your-mouth-out way that usually revealed the true character of a GF cake whenever I'd been served up fairy cakes or sponge in the past.

Dietary requirements were an important consideration of my new business, but that didn't mean I was going to sacrifice flavour or texture to fill a need for something, just to say I'd done it. There would be no sad vanilla cupcakes covered in enough frosting to sink the Titanic, and definitely no more-sugar-than-chocolate flourless brownies.

But what there might be... is gin added to the usual lemon drizzle glaze, I plotted, thinking that after the events of the past three weeks, the cake baker herself might have earned a gin or ten.

"Something smells like... burned cake?" Oliver announced, walking into the kitchen and frowning.

"First bake nerves," I explained, already busy beating the eggs for the next baking adventure. With a bit of luck, the second time would be the charm.

It needed to be because I very literally couldn't afford to keep wasting ingredients.

"I can't believe the grand opening is tomorrow. You've turned this around faster than I'd have believed possible. I'm impressed," my tennis coach informed me.

A few days had passed since the roof had been fixed and I'd used that time well, finally getting the building up to a standard I knew would pass food safety checks. Perhaps more importantly, it now looked like a place where you'd actually want to sit and drink a cup of tea whilst having a natter with your tennis pals. The house of horrors ambience had been banished.

Oliver was being a bit overenthusiastic calling tomorrow's debut a 'grand opening'. There was no big launch plan in place. I just needed to start serving and hope for the best. Every day the cafe didn't open was a day I was losing money.

"After getting the loan approved, I needed to get my skates on," I said before smiling at him. "I'm surprised, too. I think once I got going, it wasn't really as bad as all that in here. Aside from the roof, which I'm very glad has been fixed, it was just dirt and damp that had crept in. The damage was superficial. Whoever built this place did it well."

"I just thought it was a shame to see a building like this with so much character and history left to rot because of peoples' pride," Oliver agreed. "Luckily the boss man wants to protect his bottom line, and after old Roger bit the dust, I think he agreed that there needed to be some good news to balance it all out and was persuaded to stick his hand in his pocket for once. No easy feat, believe me."

I frowned at the eggs that were just starting to incorporate the air I was folding into them. "Oliver... does 'the boss man' actually have a name? Or a face?" I added, thinking I hadn't seen anyone around who'd introduced themselves as the owner of all that you see before you as far as the light touches.

"Of course he does. I just thought you knew because everyone..." He shook his head and smiled. "I keep forgetting how new you are here. You already seem like part of the scenery. That's a good thing, by the way. It means you fit in." He tilted his head. "Whether you want to be someone who fits in here is another matter." He laughed. "I'm getting distracted. He's called Gareth Dark, and he doesn't actually spend much time at the club at all because apparently there's more to his life than tennis, or something stupid like that. He probably doesn't even like cake. One of *those* people."

"That's terrible," I said, meaning it.

"Well... I'm just guessing. He seems the type who exists off meal replacement shakes and the broken spirits of the people his mega-corporation employs, chews up, and spits out."

"Sounds like a great guy."

Oliver grinned. "Good thing I've got him wrapped around my little finger. We're the best of friends. The man loves me."

"Why?" I asked before I could stop the question from leaving my lips.

True to form, Oliver didn't take the slightest bit of offence. "Because I've got the gift of charm. You've seen it in action, but you'll never know the secret." He puffed out his chest and flipped his blonde hair back, looking like an over-stuffed peacock.

"I certainly haven't noticed anything charming about you," I muttered before folding the eggs into my already creamed butter, sugar, almond and polenta mix. It already looked beautiful and I hadn't even added the lemons yet.

"That's because you don't appreciate what a fine art it is," he said cheerfully. "What are you going to call this place anyway?"

I stopped stirring and realised I hadn't got around to considering that further. And I was supposed to be opening tomorrow!

"I've got another idea," Oliver said - not surprising me in the slightest. "How about... *You Got Served! Cafe?*"

I turned the mixer up a little higher, wishing the sound could drown his words out after they had already left his mouth.

"Or, you know... you could be boring and call it the *Courtside Cafe*, or something like that," he added over the whirr of the machine.

I turned it off. The mixture was a perfect bright yellow and the smell of the lemon juice and zest I'd just added filled the air around us, banishing the last stubborn burnt notes of deadly Victoria sponge. "That is actually a nice name."

"Always the tone of surprise!" Oliver protested, but I knew he was secretly pleased I'd liked the idea he'd surely been most serious about all along. I wondered if my very limited budget would stretch to getting a sign made, or if I'd have to figure out some alternative route... maybe featuring Papier-mâché. I snorted out loud at the thought of Fillyfield Tennis Club's esteemed members being forced to look at a kids' craft sign. Whilst the idea had some appeal, I'd probably do better waiting until I could afford something a little bit more in keeping with the club's ideals.

"Do you reckon the police have given up trying to find out who did for old Roger?" Oliver asked, not changing his tone of voice in the slightest.

I shot him a warning look that he should really be careful about expressing how little he'd liked Roger. "I don't think they've given up," I said, remembering my strange encounter with DCI Pepper. "There just isn't enough evidence to point to anyone in particular. I know people still talk about the robbery theory, but I don't know..."

"You think it's more personal?"

"Don't you?" I asked Oliver, genuinely curious as to what he truly thought about the matter. I bit my lip when I reminded myself that he could still be in the running for being the person responsible for Roger's demise. After all - the one wielding the racket had either shown remarkable power or remarkable anger. Possibly both.

"Are you really still having doubts about me?" my tennis coach asked, looking torn between amusement and bemusement. "Let's be honest... do you really think I'm the type to snap and murder someone when I am a man who enjoys arguing with words, not actions? Have you ever heard me not want to have the last word in a friendly debate? And having the last word means that they get to remember how smart you are and how dumb they are. Ending an argument with a tennis racket and covering up the evidence with a ton of misdirection just doesn't carry the same satisfaction. I'm a straightforward guy. If I have a problem with you, I tell you... at great length."

He cleared his throat. "In any case, DCI Pepper told me that Roger was attacked from behind, so he didn't have a chance to fight back. The first blow would have stunned him and the rest... well, the rest finished the job." He lifted both palms upwards and looked imploringly at me, asking me if I really thought it sounded like something he would do.

In all honesty, I agreed with him. It wasn't Oliver's style, but that could also be exactly the reason why it *was* him... because he was smart enough to be aware of his own habits and know how to break them when necessary.

"I'm really not that clever," the tennis coach claimed, reading my suspicions straight off my face. "Hitting someone from behind with a tennis racket is like the sports equivalent of stabbing them in the back. If you ask me, this was someone's idea of revenge, or retribution for a time when Roger stabbed them in the back. And I can think of three people close to the scene of the crime who would fit that description."

"He stabbed you in the back, too, with that line call," I pointed out, thinking the number should be four.

"Yes, but I had it out with him right there and then and nearly got us both kicked out of the club. It's the others you want to be worrying about. They've been repressing everything. They should all take a leaf out of my book and not take any nonsense, and if someone tries to give you some nonsense, tell them you're not going to take it," he advised.

"I really do wonder why some parents let you coach their children," I sniped, but I knew I was smiling. I just couldn't help it. There was something ridiculous, and yet, strangely logical about Oliver. In truth, I thought I believed him. This wasn't about a match where he'd made a bad line call... this was something worse. Something that had triggered a reaction that had motivated someone to commit murder.

I bit my lip, thinking about the rumours of a business deal gone wrong again. Chris had been so reluctant to open up on the topic. All fingers seemed to be pointing towards the man who'd almost been my boyfriend. "Oh no," I breathed right after I slid the cake into the oven. "Fingers..."

"You forgot to add fingers to the cake?" Oliver asked, looking at me like I'd gone slightly mad.

"No... I just thought of something." My mind raced as the possibility danced in front of me tantalisingly. *Is that the reason why?* I wondered, before giving the idea up as hopeless. The tennis grip would surely be long gone by now. Unless...

"We were all searched by the police on the day of the murder, weren't we?" I asked Oliver.

He leaned against the counter and looked into the oven, watching the cake begin to rise. "Unless my police guy was particularly handsy, I assume it happened to everyone."

I nodded. The police had been very careful to search bags and give us all a good pat down to check that no one was carrying anything incriminating. I wasn't sure if they'd been looking for anything specific at the time, but it would have been very foolish indeed for the person responsible for murder to have left any obvious clue about their person. The police had then conducted a general search of the club's premises, which ruled out any casual throwing away of anything. But that didn't mean the guilty party hadn't since been back to remove any hidden evidence.

It was another lost cause. Anything that could convict the killer would be long gone.

"I've got some gossip that will cheer you up," Oliver announced, resting his head on his hand coquettishly.

I frowned at the cake in the oven. It was actually looking pretty good already. "Shouldn't you be coaching someone?"

The hint was lost on Oliver.

"I've got some free time," he cheerfully announced before continuing. "So, I heard Louise has already got herself a new doubles partner after the drama between her and Chris at the Aces on Court tournament yesterday."

"What drama?" I asked, before immediately regretting it. I hadn't wanted to know anything about the tournament after pushing Louise forward in my place and washing my hands of the whole thing.

I hadn't been incredibly surprised when Chris didn't bother to talk to me again after my substitution. Some relationships burn up with a bright, destructive flame, but some fizzle out with barely a whisper. Whatever spark there'd once been between us, it hadn't stood the test of time and the first few hurdles. I'd been silently licking my wounds in the days since I'd figured that out, trying not to think too hard about what the mixed doubles pair would be getting up to, but it seemed as though I wasn't going to be given a free pass.

13

OLD HABITS

"So get this..." Oliver said, jumping straight into his stride. "They managed to beat their opponents in the first round, but as soon as they left the court, the man on the other team had a problem with Chris. The way I heard it, there was some accusation of match fixing. He alleged that Chris had charmed his female opponent and promised her something in return for not bringing her best effort."

"Did she admit that was the case?" Even though I'd told myself it was time to let Chris go, the idea of him schmoozing with other women, and in such a manipulative way, was like a punch to the gut.

"Of course not, but that didn't stop everything from kicking off. The match loser realised words weren't getting him anywhere, so he used his fists. Chris claimed he was only defending himself when he hit the other guy over the head with a - wait for it - tennis racket." Oliver raised his eyebrows, wanting me to join the dots. "But I'm sure that was just a coincidence and definitely not something he'd ever used as a weapon before."

"Okay, I get the picture," I said, thinking that amount of sarcasm was hardly necessary. I knew it didn't look good for Chris. Especially when I had my suspicions about the reason why a certain piece of evidence had gone missing.

"Obviously, that got all of them kicked out of the Aces on Court tournament and banned from ever returning. All in all, you definitely made the right call to duck out. Having said that, I still think you'd have done pretty well. With a better partner," he added and then laughed as something else jumped into his head. "I also heard that Louise batted her eyelashes at the tournament organiser and managed to get herself excluded from the ban, saying she'd had no part in the alleged bribery. She stayed to watch the rest of the competition and waited to find out who the winners were, before making herself very friendly with the male half of the winning team. I guess Louise is already planning ahead for next year's tournament." He grinned at me.

I took a moment to wonder if everybody around here suffered from the same alarming lack of empathy, as they all seemed to bounce back from major upsets remarkably quickly. Perhaps that was the way you needed to be when you were someone who'd clawed their way through others in order to summit the mountain of success. You focused on yourself and anything that took time away from you getting what you wanted was a distraction.

"I don't understand how Louise can move on so quickly when she told me over and over how much she loved Roger," I commented.

Oliver nodded. "Oh, sure... but it's like I told you. I think she enjoyed the sympathy that came with being romantically entangled with a pest like Roger. With Roger gone and the sympathy over his demise drying up, she's back to her old ways of trying to use relationships to get ahead in life. After

Chris dropped the ball, she decided to move on up in the world. History repeating itself," he added with a shrug.

"History…" I said, wondering why that word was chiming with me right now. This whole club was steeped in the stuff! Even the clubhouse had a past I had not sought to cover up when I'd cleaned up and redecorated. There had been a few necessary updates. I'd had to put some of the loan money towards some new tables and chairs, as many had gone missing over the years and others were beyond resurrection. I'd also purchased some strawberry-themed tablecloths and cushions to tie the mishmash of furniture together in a way that made me think of a cosy living room rather than a uniform cafeteria. But behind the newly painted walls and the up-cycled furnishings, the lustrous backdrop of what had been there before remained - a reminder of a tennis club with a strong pedigree.

And it was in that history I suddenly felt sure the answer to the mystery of Roger Riley's death resided.

"How good are you at breaking-into places where you shouldn't be?" I asked Oliver.

His grin was as wide as I'd ever seen it. "I'm very good," he said, confirming what I'd already guessed from his tales of snooping around in the club owner's office.

"Then I have a job for you."

The first locker we broke into was Roger's.

It was empty.

Oliver had mentioned the rusty old lockers the first time he'd shown me the clubhouse. They'd been covered with a dust sheet back then and I'd left it in place, not sparing a thought for the dark corner that no one seemed to visit.

"Maybe I'm wrong about this," I muttered as Oliver twisted two bendy pieces of metal in the lock of the locker that collectively belonged to the umpires of Fillyfield. He was alarmingly efficient and the door popped open without much of a fight. Inside were ancient scorecards and an apple so shrivelled and shrunken it could be put in a museum as an ancient artifact.

"Does Chris have one?" I asked, already feeling the answer settle in my stomach like a lead weight.

"His family have been here for generations, so... yes, but not under his last name. I believe there was some sort of family breakup at some point and names were swapped," Oliver, fountain of all tennis club gossip, informed me.

"Which also means that even if the police did casually cast their eye over the lockers and open any belonging to those involved, they'd probably have missed it," I concluded, wondering just how public the knowledge of Chris's name change was and if the police had even looked at the row of rusted boxes beneath the white veil of fabric. I doubted it.

"This is probably a waste of time," I said as Oliver scanned the faded nameplates before finally alighting on the one that allegedly belonged to Chris's family. "You said no one uses these, right?"

My tennis coach with a suspicious amount of experience in picking locks stopped in the middle of levering open the legacy locker and looked up at me. "It's true that these lockers are largely junk and having one is just for the prestige. I mean... they're not exactly secure. One key will open any of them." He twisted the pieces of metal and the lock squeaked before the levers lifted and the door opened, proving his point.

This locker wasn't empty.

A bright yellow grip, clearly used and removed from a tennis racket stared back at us. Next to it lay a diamond ring that flashed in the daylight that crept past us into the locker.

"That does not look good," Oliver said stating the obvious.

"It doesn't look good at all," DCI Pepper said from where

she'd just opened the door to the clubhouse and walked in to find us in the middle of breaking into lockers.

"It's not what it looks like," Oliver announced, making a bad situation worse as he proceeded to drop his lock-picking kit on the floor with a loud clang.

We stood with the open locker door and its suspicious contents directly in-between us.

"What brings you here on this fine day, DCI Pepper?" Oliver enquired when the silence seemed charged enough to explode.

If this was his famous charm, it needed some work.

DCI Pepper glared at him. "I was here to ask Ms Perry some more questions about her whereabouts prior to Roger Riley's murder, but I think this sheds some new light on it."

We all turned and looked at the contents of the locker.

"It's not *my* locker," Oliver hastily interjected, doing everything he could to wriggle out of the situation.

"And obviously I don't have a locker here at the tennis club," I added, glaring at my partner in crime.

"That seems obvious, as it looks very much as though you were breaking-in to plant evidence in a locker that belongs to someone else. And that is a very grave offence indeed. Especially when you pair it with missing evidence that is likely to play a vital role in convicting the person responsible for the murder of Roger Riley. I knew I'd catch you redhanded one day, Serena Perry. You are a criminal through and through, and now I finally have the proof."

"What?!" I protested, looking back and forth between the locker and the DCI.

DCI Pepper let her breath go in a sudden sigh. "But... while you clearly have no regard for people's private property, I don't think you're a murderer. Not this time, anyway," she added, using the prospect of me one day slipping up and murdering someone to cheer herself up. "Luckily for you, I actually arrived here ten minutes ago and witnessed you opening two other lockers before you tried this one. I know that those things were already in the locker when you opened it up. And I think the evidence speaks for itself."

"It does," I agreed before biting my lip and looking once again at the yellow grip and seeing a few indentations - just as I'd suspected there might be once I'd spent time considering why someone would go to so much trouble to conceal a racket grip when fingerprints were so easily wiped off.

"The question is... where do we go from here?" DCI Pepper said, rubbing her chin thoughtfully. "With so many lawyers floating around the place, I need a confession. And there's only one way I can think to get it." Her mouth twisted with displeasure as she considered the distasteful idea.

I crossed my arms and waited for her to ask for a favour she really didn't want to ask for. But even in as grave a situation as this one, I was going to make her say it.

"I could do with your help," the DCI finally confessed, looking as if she'd have rather licked a frog than uttered those words.

"And I'll be happy to help," I replied, ready to enter a truce - even after the way DCI Pepper had tried to paint me with a criminal brush again. "Right after I take the cake out of the oven," I added a split second before the timer went off... my cooking senses proving they were still with me in the uncanny way they always had been. Everyone has quirks they can't explain. This was my tiny talent. It was a gift I used without even thinking about it, but it had saved many a cake when a timer had let me down. My extra sense never failed.

Excluding Victoria sponges.

"And I'll be happy to help as well... after a slice of cake," Oliver added, even though no one had asked him.

DCI Pepper shot him a glare, confirming that he was definitely no longer her favourite person at Fillyfield Tennis

Club. After the stress this case had caused the DCI, she probably hoped she'd never again have to hear the words 'tennis' or 'murder' in the same sentence. That was a sentiment we shared.

"Or now! I can help right now," Oliver hastily amended, folding under the intensity of the warning look. He clapped his hands together and grinned. "It sounds like I've got a tennis match to organise..."

14

REMATCH

I t was drizzling when I met Oliver on court the next morning. We'd agreed to get there fifteen minutes earlier than the allotted time he'd given for what was supposed to be the Roger Riley memorial match. At first, I'd assumed that the other three would refuse to play, considering it in poor taste to essentially hold the match we'd planned to play on the day Roger had died - only with Oliver standing in for the dead man.

I should have known the thought wouldn't even cross their minds - especially when Oliver had added that it should be a charity match that could be publicised in the next club newsletter. It was all in memory of the man who'd passed away and would be - Oliver had taken care to emphasise - so greatly missed by all of us.

I'd bitten my nails in the background each time he'd made the phone call to Harry, Chris, and Louise, expecting them to see through the ruse. Everybody had replied saying that they'd love to be involved in such a well-publicised charitable effort. And wasn't it terrible how it was now clear that Roger had been murdered by opportunist thieves who'd stolen valuables before making their getaway, never to be seen again? It was a tragedy that no one could have predicted or stopped, Oliver had said, feeding them all the lines they wanted to hear.

I'd thought it was the most obvious trap in the world, but the call of a charitable act and old habits dying hard were enough to make them blind to the obvious. Or perhaps it was simply a case of the killer believing they had got away with murder.

"I have a question," Oliver said in a tone of voice that heavily implied it probably wasn't going to be a very serious question.

"Yes, I brought the cake I baked yesterday - even though you tried to eat it as soon as it came out of the oven. And I'm glad you burned yourself on the tin. I hope it taught you a valuable lesson." I pulled a face, wondering why I sounded like I was talking to a badly behaved five-year-old. Actually, a five-year-old would have learned a valuable lesson, but Oliver seemed to be someone who delighted in finding things out the hard way... and then repeating the same action.

"Good to know, but not what I was going to ask," he claimed. "Do you think we could actually play some doubles before getting to the other stuff? Lately, there seems to have been a lot of drama and not enough tennis. A few good serves from me... you put away some volleys... we leave the court with a criminal in our clutches, but with the added benefit of knowing that we would have definitely trashed them if the match had gone ahead."

"No!" a disembodied voice shouted from somewhere deep inside a hedgerow.

I smirked at Oliver but had to wipe it off my face a second later when the sound of footsteps approaching down the sandy path heralded the arrival of the other players.

It was time for the game to begin.

"Good morning, good morning," Chris said, stepping out onto the court and nodding at Oliver before sort of looking past me, rather than at me.

Louise snorted audibly before rolling her eyes at me. Clearly Chris was not flavour of the month with her either after the terrible tournament. "Do we really have to play as these teams? I think it would be better if I went with Oliver," she suggested as Harry sidled past and climbed the steps to the umpire's chair.

"Well, I think it would be best if *I* played with Oliver," Chris cut in. "What do you say? How about a good old fashioned boys-versus-girls?"

If I'd needed any more confirmation of how the spark had fled from whatever relationship I'd imagined there to be between us, that was it.

"My, my… I've never been so popular," Oliver said, apparently lapping up all the attention - even though he knew the underlying reasons behind what was being said. "But the teams are final," he added with a sympathetic smile I knew was fake. He was loving watching the other team tear themselves apart.

I suddenly regretted the order that we weren't allowed to play any actual tennis. It would have felt pretty good to wipe the smile off Chris's face after the extra work Oliver and I had put in every moment we'd both had spare over the past few days. When we'd played a few points at the end of the lessons he'd even lost a few. Normally, I'd have been left in some doubt as to whether he'd been giving it his all or if it was a case of the coach letting the student win a few points to boost their confidence, but when Oliver lost a point, the amount of cursing and amateur dramatics let you know he'd genuinely made a mistake. Plus, I was well aware that Oliver was not exactly the type to cushion the reality of how badly you sucked - whether you were five-years-old or fifty.

I cleared my throat to speak. "I think we should all have a moment of silence for Roger, whose life was cut short..." I took a breath. "...by someone that he thought he could trust."

All of the heads nodding in agreement stopped.

"What? I thought the police decided it was a random robbery?" Louise said, looking confused. Her puzzlement appeared to be shared amongst the group, but I knew there was a killer in our midst.

"Everyone was starting to think that way... right up until the missing tennis grip turned up," Oliver chimed in.

"Turned up?" Harry queried, his forehead lining with concern. "Where did it turn up?"

"Inside one of the lockers in the clubhouse," Oliver answered. "It looks as though the person responsible for Roger's death stashed the grip in their locker after committing the crime."

"Wouldn't anyone with an ounce of common sense go back and dispose of the evidence afterwards?" Chris asked, frowning very believably.

"Probably," I agreed, "but it might have been tough when the club house suddenly had someone spending an awful lot of time in there." I indicated myself. "I also think ego played a fairly big part in this crime. The person responsible believed they'd got away with it, so they left the evidence locked up," I added.

"Whose locker was it in?" Chris pressed, looking frustrated.

"Yours," Oliver informed him, watching his face for a reaction.

Chris turned white before colour rushed back into his face. "What? That's not possible! I don't... I don't even use that old family thing! I don't think I even have a key. Who uses those lockers anyway? They're junk!"

Louise and Harry looked at him like he'd sprouted another head.

"You don't honestly think that I...?" Chris's voice turned strangled at the end of a sentence he seemed unable to finish. "Look, if all this is true, you would have gone to the police!"

"We wanted to give the killer a chance to explain themselves first," Oliver told him, already prepared for that question.

"When we found the grip, it was immediately clear why the killer had decided to conceal it. And it had nothing to do with fingerprints," I jumped back in, ignoring Chris's stuttering. "Show me your hands, please."

In a daze, he flipped both hands palm-side up.

"You're wearing rings. They must make marks on the grip of your racket. Especially if you're holding the racket in one position and delivering a lot of force." I mimed the movement that had been used to dispatch Roger. "And having marks like that on a grip would be more obvious than fingerprints, which were carefully removed from the racket."

"This is ridiculous. What reason would I have had to want to do that to Roger?" Chris said, having recovered from the initial shock of being accused.

"The grip wasn't the only thing that was in your family's locker," I told him. "There was also a ring. That business deal that went wrong was over counterfeit jewellery, wasn't it?" I held my breath, knowing I'd just made my first big gamble.

Chris hadn't wanted to talk about the deal in any kind of specifics, but I was going off rumours and something Harry had implied about Roger's penchant for fake flashy things and how those fakes were good enough to fool all kinds of people.

When a dark cloud came over Chris's face, I knew I'd struck gold. Or in this case... fool's gold.

"No wonder you were angry with Roger. You believed that he was responsible for trying to fob you off with fakes. But I'll bet good money that the diamond ring in your locker is the real deal."

"*Diamond* ring?" Chris said numbly.

Oliver raised his eyebrows at the accused. "I'm sure you always suspected that Roger had double-crossed you deliberately. Maybe you even thought he'd done some switching around. You told me yourself that Roger liked to get his hands on whatever it was he was selling. Surely he of all people would have known a fake from the real deal... unless he was the one responsible for the fakes."

"It was a genuine supply chain error and we claimed off our business insurance," Chris muttered, shaking his head in disbelief.

"Maybe you wanted to believe that... until Roger brought out the ring and told you about his plan to propose to Louise. He'd already told Harry, so it would make sense that he'd share it with the other member of such a closely knit friendship group," I jumped in. "You may have let the business deal go, but seeing that ring brought all of that anger back, tipping you over the edge."

"What proposal? I never..." Chris spluttered.

"I can't believe he was going to propose!" Louise said, tears coursing down her cheeks. Harry moved to her side, wrapping a comforting arm across her shoulders. She turned towards him and he wrapped her in an embrace, his mouth set in a grim line as he looked accusingly at his friend.

"I can't believe you're trying to pin this on me," Chris jumped back in, looking furious enough to start hitting things with a tennis racket. "If all this is true, why haven't you called the police? I'm not giving you an explanation for something I haven't done!"

"The truth is, we only found the grip and the ring right before you all arrived," Oliver said, spinning the lie we'd been asked to tell. "We'll call the police soon, but after everything we've been through together and the way we've all been under suspicion - not to mention the betrayal of friendship - I think we're all owed a proper explanation." He looked across at me, giving me a silent cue.

"It's time to come clean for the sake of your friends and ask for forgiveness." I turned my back on Chris. "What do you say, Harry?"

The umpire froze. "What do I say to what?"

Oliver moved to stand next to me. "Will you tell us all why you murdered Roger and then tried to pin it on Chris?"

Harry's mouth gold-fished for a few seconds, but the fear that had flashed behind his eyes the moment that the accusation had been levelled at him was all that any of us had needed to see.

"Why would I do something like that?" he protested even as Louise slipped out of his embrace and moved several metres away, clutching herself and looking lost. "I didn't have any business deals with Roger, and the worst he'd ever done to me was taking that embarrassing photo - which I told you all about! It's hardly a good reason to kill someone. I think you made it pretty clear how Chris had the most to lose in this situation. You found a ring and the missing grip in his locker!"

"Both things that you put there," I said. "As Oliver proved when we broke into the lockers, they're not exactly secure. In fact, it turns out the keys are all the same. Someone with the key to the umpire's locker would have access to all of the others, which is probably why no one actually uses them. I think you hoped the police would search the lockers immediately after the crime. That way you'd have got rid of both Chris and Roger... your two rivals out of the race."

Harry shook his head and even managed to force a laugh. "Now you're saying I had it in for Chris, too? Why? We're friends! What has Chris ever done to me? Or Roger, for that matter..."

I looked towards Oliver, hoping he would step in and take over, but his mouth suddenly looked permanently zipped shut.

I took a deep breath before addressing Harry again. "How long have you been in love with Louise?"

"What?" Louise exclaimed, her eyes growing wide. "That's not true! We're friends and nothing has ever happened between us. Isn't that right, Harry?"

"Right," he agreed, holding my gaze like a fox caught in a trap.

"Louise, haven't you ever wondered why Harry was always the umpire at your matches? I saw the court reservation sheets ages ago, and there it was, plain as day... I just didn't know what I was looking at," I explained. "It was only when we found the grip and the ring that the pieces finally slotted together and the real story emerged. Harry... you were the one who told me that you thought the racket grip could have been taken for reasons other than fingerprints, which got me thinking about why it might have gone missing. That led me to suspect that there was something about the grip that would give away the identity of the killer - just as you planned when I presume you marked up the grip after the murder using the very ring that Roger must have revealed to you at the same time he told you he was planning to propose to Louise. It was a proposal that only you knew about - but you mentioned it to me when we spoke on court together," I reminded him.

"You said the diamond in the ring was proof of Roger

cheating Chris on the business deal. It's obvious, isn't it?" Harry protested.

"While the deal did go pear-shaped, it sounds like with business insurance no harm was actually done. And who knows if Roger really was responsible for the fakes," Oliver said, glancing at Chris, who just shrugged and continued to look shellshocked. "It was the ring which triggered your violent reaction because you knew once and for all that Louise would be out of reach. You'd tried so hard to win her over as the years passed, hoping she'd turn your way when Roger was always running off with other women."

"But she turned to Chris instead… and those were matches that didn't need an umpire," I added, bringing up the games the pair had played on Wednesday nights when the courts were otherwise empty. "It's no wonder you had no qualms at all about trying to frame your friend for murder when you were struck by the same jealousy you'd felt when Roger announced out of the blue that he was going to propose to Louise. You even gave Louise a necklace with a meaningful message on it, didn't you?" I said, suddenly inspired by a recollection of the necklace in question and the phrase inscribed on the back - a confession that a ball had been on the line when he'd probably called it in favour of one of his friends - the way Louise had claimed Harry tended to. "Only… Louise never realised how you felt. That necklace was more than an apology and everything else you did to be near her was also more than it seemed."

"Is any of this true?" Louise asked, turning to Harry with her blue eyes wide. "Do you feel that way about me?"

15

STRAWBERRIES AND CREAM

"I …" Harry faltered, his repressed feelings getting the better of him. "I don't know what to say," he confessed, still fixed on Louise. "I just wanted to be there for you, always."

"But you never said anything!"

"I thought you knew!" he said, his voice cracking. "I mean, isn't it obvious? Every match, I was there. Every time Roger ran off with another woman, I was there for you. I told you to just forget about him a thousand times, but when you finally seemed to be thinking there could be more than Roger out there… you ran to Chris. I knew it was just to make Roger jealous, but why couldn't you have given me a chance? I'd have done everything for you. I *did* everything for you," he added quietly.

He shook his head. "I couldn't let you tie yourself to a man like Roger forever, so when he told me about his plan to propose to you - which he was only doing in order to make sure you forgot about Chris - I knew what I had to do. I picked up one of his rackets when his back was turned and put an end to Roger's cruel ways once and for all. It was only afterwards that I realised what I'd done. That was when I panicked. I suppose instinct took over and my mind was fixed on Chris the same way Roger's had been. I used the engagement ring to mark the grip as if someone with rings on their fingers had committed the crime and I wiped down the racket. I thought about just leaving it there, but it didn't feel like it was enough. What if the police saw it as a set up? What sort of fool would leave evidence that obvious lying around? The lockers jumped into my head. I thought the police would search the whole club and I figured that if they found the ring, too, they'd probably assume that Chris was the one who was upset over the proposal, or something like that, as he and Louise had been spending so much time alone together. I didn't know that the thing between them was already over until you turned up on the morning of the match," he said, gesturing to me before shaking his head. "I doubt Roger knew either, which was why he was going ahead with his big proposal plan. Finding all of that in Chris's family's locker would have looked really bad, and hopefully the details would be glossed over. Clearly, I expected too much of the police."

Anger flashed across his face for a second - a horrible jealousy that twisted his features. "I've always been the better choice, Louise. Always." He sighed. "If I'd been thinking straight, I should have taken Roger's fake Rolex and gold chains and got rid of the grip and the ring for good. Then the police could have stuck to their random robbery theory and everything would have been fine. Maybe then..." He looked hopefully at Louise, but there was no warmth returned.

"I can't believe you'd do this. I thought we were friends," Louise said, shrinking back even further from the umpire. I suddenly recalled Louise's words about no one wanting to be her friend for the sake of friendship. Tragically, it would appear that she had been right about that all along.

Harry just looked at her with the expression of a broken man before turning his despondent gaze on the rest of us. "I suppose you'll be calling the police now. I'm not telling them anything without my lawyer. All of this is circumstantial. They have nothing on me," he added, his expression changing as he started to consider how much trouble he'd got himself into.

"We didn't think you'd be likely to cooperate once you were in custody," a voice from the hedgerow said before a hawthorn bush wobbled menacingly. "That's why we set up this match and recorded everything!"

There was the sound of cloth ripping followed by some muffled cursing.

A second later, DCI Pepper fell flat on her face on the tennis-court side of the hedge, her ankles snagged by the prickly bush.

Harry gave a squeak of alarm upon seeing the DCI.

"Was that the signal, Ma'am?" someone called from inside another bush further down the field.

"Yes! Arrest him!" DCI Pepper ordered from her undignified position on the grass, trying to fight off the clutches of the hawthorn.

Harry was already sprinting away across the courts, heading for the gate on the far side that led to more fields and woods.

"Really?" I muttered in disbelief. He couldn't possibly believe he'd get far.

"Shouldn't someone run after him?" Chris suggested, doing his usual thing of putting an idea forward but making it clear that he certainly wasn't going to be the one to act on it.

Louise was quietly having a dramatic meltdown that for once no one was paying attention to.

I glanced at Oliver, but he was already helping himself to

a slice of the cake I'd brought along with the intention that he could have it after the job had been done.

"What? He's not going to get far! There's a good reason why Harry's an umpire and not a player. The man can't run for peanuts," Oliver said right as Harry made it to the gate and threw it open, before attempting to jump the hedge. "I mean, the whole running away thing is ridiculous. Where does he think he's going?" he added when Harry picked himself up from the ill-advised hedge vault and dashed haphazardly through the field of maize beyond. By now the police officers had managed to extricate themselves from their hiding places. It wasn't long before three officers dressed in dark blue were chasing Harry through the field as he zig-zagged back and forth.

I sat down on the bench next to Oliver, watching as the chase unfolded. He was right. We'd done our bit. It was time to let the authorities do their part.

"Cake?" Oliver suggested. I accepted the slice he held out for me to take. "Anyone else?" he added, but Chris and Louise just stared into the distance at nothing, their world shaken to pieces. "How could you have ever been interested in someone who doesn't like cake?" Oliver said, quietly enough that only I could hear it.

A hand reached down and took a slice from the box. To my astonishment, I discovered it belonged to DCI Pepper - who appeared to be bleeding from multiple scratch wounds. If I'd been asked to make a decision on who won the fight, I would have awarded it to the hedge.

"Got him!" one of the officers shouted from the field as the other two flung themselves on hapless Harry.

"My lawyer will..." he started to say, but the police officer just cut him off by reminding him they had a full confession on tape, and even the best lawyer in the world was going to struggle to fight that one.

"Huh…" DCI Pepper said after taking a giant bite of the cake as the murderer was handcuffed. She looked down at the gin-infused lemon polenta loaf with a thoughtful expression. "You know what… maybe you are a real baker after all."

"I did try to tell you," I couldn't resist sniping, frustrated by how many times the DCI had tried to trip me up and convict me of crimes I hadn't committed. The proof had very literally been in the pudding all along.

DCI Pepper took another bite and shook her head, looking as solemn and serious as I'd ever seen. Was my cake really that life changing? I waited to see if she was going to add a compliment - something that might lay the foundation of an accord between us that I hoped would spring from the way we'd collaborated today.

"This means… you're a smarter criminal than I thought," she said, narrowing her eyes at the cake. "You nearly had me convinced for a second, but I know a coverup when I see one. I'll catch you out one day, Serena Perry."

I shot an exasperated look at Oliver, who was unhelpfully grinning from ear to ear.

"Thank you for your valuable service to keeping our community safe," he told DCI Pepper with the utmost sincerity.

"Nice try, but I've witnessed your criminal behaviour firsthand. It's obvious you're working together. I'll be keeping a close eye on you both," she replied.

Now it was my turn to shoot Oliver a smug smile.

"It's so nice that you're going to be taking an interest in my life. It's all I've ever wanted," Oliver replied, pretending to wipe a tear away as he took it in his stride the way he seemed to take everything.

"Well… just watch your step," DCI Pepper added, the wind taken out of her sails by his weird response.

"I certainly will," the tennis coach assured her before picking up the cakebox. "More cake, DCI Pepper?"

A small internal battle took place. She reached out and accepted a second piece.

"Happy opening day!" Oliver said, reminding me what this day was supposed to be.

"Maybe it should be postponed," I mused, thinking of everything that had just happened and how most people probably wouldn't be in the mood to pop in to a new cafe in the wake of one of the tennis club's own members being revealed as a coldblooded killer whose jealousy had got the better of him.

"You can't postpone life," Oliver said thoughtfully. His usual smile suddenly took hold of his tanned face. "Besides... I already invited the whole club, and I know you've been up baking since the break of dawn. And even I can't eat that much cake."

"You could try," I said with a sideways smile.

"I could definitely try," he agreed, but he'd persuaded me. The Courtside Cafe would open, even if it was a damp squib.

It just went to show how much I'd misjudged human nature.

When the Courtside Cafe officially opened its doors at 4pm that afternoon, it seemed like the whole club had turned out for the occasion. The terrace and the veranda filled up with people and I was rushed off my feet serving cakes and cream teas. Gossip floated on the air and the morning's drama was not far from anyone's lips.

"Told you it was the perfect day for it," Oliver said, lounging next to the bar and helping himself to a plate of green-coloured coconut macaroons I'd decorated with white chocolate to look like tennis balls. "People like good news, but they *love* bad news. Almost as much as I love cake," he added, smiling a green smile,

I tried not to laugh. Perhaps I'd used too much food colouring. "Be that as it may, I hope it's the last bad news we have for a long time. It would be nice to live a drama free life," I said wistfully.

"If you wanted drama free... you're in the wrong sport," Oliver cheerfully informed me. "It's not all strawberries and cream. There's racket breaking, dodgy line calls, saying rude things to the umpire..."

"Sometimes there's even some tennis," I added drily.

Oliver grinned more greenly than ever. "Occasionally... but let's be honest, the best part about tennis is not actually the tennis. It's the on-court drama."

I considered that statement. "I think I need a new tennis coach."

EPILOGUE

"**U**nk!" I said, or something to that effect. It was more of a sound than a word that left my mouth when the ball gave me a glancing blow to the shoulder.

"Never take your eye off the ball!" Oliver yelled from the other side of the net.

"You told me to look over at the other court!" I yelled back - no longer a passive student who would blindly follow the words of her coach, but someone who now had opinions of their own on all things tennis.

"I did... but didn't I also tell you to never trust your opponent?"

I stood up straight and stuck my hands on my hips. "You said that too... right after you told me to always trust your tennis coach."

Oliver scratched his head. "That is a paradox, isn't it?"

I took the opportunity to take a ball out of my pocket and shoot it back over the net at him.

"Hey!" he said as he was forced to snake out of the way. The next one I'd hit right after the first bounced off his chest.

"Always expect the unexpected," I quoted at him.

"Which idiot taught you to play tennis?" he grumbled, but I knew that he would forgive me later when it was time for coffee. He'd get first pick of the cakes on offer - as per our agreement.

Even though Oliver had said that he could only fit in these lessons whenever he had a free moment, our early morning hits had become something of a habit. The tennis club was open seven days a week and I'd decided that the best way to get into my stride was to open the cafe for all of them. The majority of the Fillyfield Tennis Club's members were not particularly early risers. They tended to drift in as the morning wore on. By the time they'd finished batting about tennis balls that looked like they dated from decades ago I was ready and waiting to welcome them to the Court-side Cafe with a warm smile and a slice of the daily special.

Oliver had been right about there being no shortage of drama at the club. A couple of days after the cafe had first opened, a group of four women in their thirties had come in after playing a morning match. They'd then proceeded to gossip loudly about how attractive that tennis coach with the interestingly dyed hair was, musing about whether he was single.

"I'm going to find out if he has any coaching slots open, although I wouldn't be surprised if he offered to teach me for free," the most confident member of the group had said just as I'd placed down the healthy option I'd baked for the diet-conscious amongst the club's members. Today, I'd made apricot and date slices that had no added sugar beyond the fruit itself. Oliver had tried them and informed me he would rather eat cardboard next time, but I'd thought they were pretty good for something a little lower in guilt.

"Do you think he does the hands-on thing, where if you're really messing up a shot, the coach comes and moves your arms through the motion?" an excitable redhead had interjected.

"I think I'd pretend to not know what I was doing just to convince him to do that!" another had swooned.

"You don't want that to happen, trust me," I'd said mildly, pushing plates in all directions for them to pick at before competing to see who could leave the most behind as they showed how virtuous they were.

"Why ever not?" the loudest of the group had enquired with such volume it made other heads in the cafe swivel in our direction - even though I'd known they'd already been listening to every word of what had happened so far.

"Don't get me wrong, Oliver is a very accomplished coach," I'd said, setting myself up for the next line. "It's a shame he's got the most terrible halitosis. It's a genuine medical condition he suffers from."

There'd been silence around the table as everyone present had tried to figure out what I was talking about. Judging by the expressions on some of their faces, we were very much not on the same page.

"Bad breath!" I'd announced just as loudly as the brunette.

The room had hastily returned to murmured conversations, but I hadn't missed the sound of someone noisily spitting their tea out in the kitchen.

It had taken a lot of cake to get Oliver to forgive me for that, and I still wasn't convinced he wasn't planning some sort of revenge. Since that day, he'd been chewing gum whenever I'd seen him - even though I had assured him it was merely an amusing joke. He'd pointed out that I might know it was false, but his street-cred with the tennis club ladies had taken a nosedive, and now it was taking a pack of chewing gum a day to restore.

I'd tried to keep a solemn expression on my face when he'd explained his predicament, but in the end, I'd had to excuse myself and make a run for the bushes where I'd then tried to stifle my laughter whilst Oliver had shouted that he knew what I was doing and that our next tennis lesson would consist of laps run repeatedly around the entire court complex.

Even after running what had felt like multiple marathons, I regretted nothing.

Aside from Oliver forcing me to run more laps whenever he imagined someone was trying to smell his breath, things had gone pretty smoothly in the wake of the terrible truth about Roger Riley's death coming out. I knew Louise and Chris were doing everything they could to avoid coming into the cafe whenever I was there, but I'd noticed they'd started rebooking their old match time together. Perhaps the tragedy had brought them closer together again, but I no longer had a strong opinion on the matter.

It was a strange thing to think, but I was grateful I'd met Chris and told the tall tale which had landed me in such trouble at the tennis club. If I hadn't enlisted Oliver's help to make me into a passable excuse for a tennis player, the opportunity to take on the clubhouse and convert it into a cafe would never have come knocking. I'd never have found myself pitching the bank for a business loan, and I'd never have been rushed off my feet serving cake and coffee. I was even seriously considering expanding into full lunches to grow my already popular business.

In the end, I liked to think that everything happened for a reason. Sometimes you had to crawl through miles of dirt to reach the pot of gold at the end of the rainbow. I frowned, suddenly wondering if Roger's terrible use of clichés had rubbed off on me.

"No! No you don't! You thieving little..." Oliver shouted in the middle of the rally that was turning into more of a tennis ball fight. He pulled more balls out of the hopper and I emptied my pockets in retaliation, sending them flying in every direction... including to the edges of the tennis court.

Oliver ducked my next volley and sprinted towards the open gate that led onto Court One, but he was already too late. Sampras gave a victorious meow and fled with his fresh victim firmly clutched in his mouth - another tennis ball fallen prey to the fearsome feline.

"Come back! Bring that back here!" Oliver demanded, tearing after the cat as Sampras became a ginger streak running through the longer grass. The tennis coach followed at full-sprint. When the cat dodged through the hedgerow, I thought Oliver would give up, but apparently this was one tennis ball too many. Or perhaps it was the fact that Sampras had brought his thieving ways onto the court itself instead of preying on stray balls that landed beyond the fences.

It was actually rather impressive to see my tennis coach clear the hedge with a single leap. Unfortunately, there was a ditch right on the other side that he didn't clear according to the loud splash and all of the rude words that followed. "Get back here!" he shouted a few moments later. I watched as he continued to give chase across the field of wheat, his smartly matching tracksuit now covered in mud up to knee height.

Sampras had managed to gain a big lead, but Oliver was spurred on by frustration and the need to achieve something after giving chase so dramatically. It was too close to call.

"My money is on the cat," one of the ladies from Court Two said as the group wandered over to watch the morning's entertainment unfold.

"I don't know... Oliver's got longer legs," another pointed out.

We all watched as the chase continued. They zig-zagged back and forth through the field - almost as if Sampras was deliberately toying with the tennis coach.

"What do you think you're doing running through my

field of wheat?!" came the cry of the outraged farmer who'd been tending the field adjacent to the one Oliver and Sampras were now in the process of ruining.

Oliver must have replied with something other than a heartfelt apology because the farmer ran to the gate between the fields, joining the chase himself and loudly threatening to wring the tennis coach's neck.

"I've got it! I've got it!" Oliver shouted two minutes later, raising a tennis ball high in the air. The farmer had got a pitchfork from somewhere and Oliver was forced to continue running.

A slightly disappointed applause broke out amongst the audience at Oliver's victory over the tennis club's cat.

I joined in, trying not to turn my head to look at the ginger shape I saw emerge from one side of the hedgerow from the corner of my eye. Sampras slunk along the side of the court and seized a tennis ball that had escaped during our furious tennis ball battle. I couldn't help but wonder if that was the ball the cat had planned to steal all along.

With Oliver still celebrating his victory whilst being chased by a furious farmer, Sampras trotted off into the bushes after another successful hunt.

"Never take your eye off the ball!" Oliver advised us all, ducking a swing of the pitchfork and making a break for it through the open gate with the farmer still cursing him.

It was too bad Oliver had been watching the wrong ball.

RECIPE FOR COFFEE AND WALNUT CAKE

Coffee and walnut cake is one of the most popular and comforting cakes ever made. It comes with the benefit of looking impressive, so is a great one to whip up when you're expecting company!

The cake on the cover of this book features a glaze rather than buttercream (and it's beautiful!) but I am much more partial to what I'd call a traditional coffee and walnut cake. This is one of my all-time favourite recipes. Every year my dad requests it for his birthday - so you know it's a good cake!

Ingredients:

For the cake:

- 225g butter
- 225g caster sugar
- 4 large eggs
- 2 heaped tsps of coffee granules dissolved in 50ml

water or a couple of espresso shots from a coffee maker
- 225g self-raising flour
- 75g walnuts chopped plus some halves for decoration

For the buttercream icing:

- 125g unsalted butter
- 225g icing sugar
- 3 tsps of coffee granules dissolved in 1 tsp of water, or a strong espresso

Method:

Start by preheating the oven to 180C/350F/Gas 4. Prepare two 20cm/8 inch cake tins by greasing or lining with baking parchment.

Beat the butter and sugar together until creamed. They should look light and fluffy!

Start adding the eggs one at a time. Make sure you beat well and incorporate each egg before adding the next. If you think the mix is on the cusp of curdling, add a spoon of your flour and continue. Once you've incorporated the eggs, add the dissolved coffee or strong espresso.

Fold in the flour and combine, adding the walnuts last so they don't get too crushed. A chunky texture is great in a cake!

Divide your mixture between your two pre-prepared tins. Pop them in the oven to bake for 25-30 minutes, or until a skewer pushed into the middle of the cake comes out clean and the cake is golden and springy to touch. Take them out of the oven and leave to cool. You can turn them out onto a wire rack at this stage.

In the meantime, it's a great idea to make your butter-cream! Start by beating the butter until its become pale and looks smooth with no buttery lumps remaining. Next, add the icing sugar and continue to beat before finally adding the dissolved coffee or espresso shot.

Whilst you want the icing to have that beautiful coffee flavour (and you should definitely taste test for this!) be wary of watering down the icing too much. Try to make your espresso as strong as you can with as little liquid as possible.

When your cake has fully cooled, divide the icing in half. Spread the first lot on top of one of the sponges and sandwich with the other sponge. Use the rest of the icing to cover the top of your cake (leaving the sides bare, but beautiful to look at!) and finally decorate with halved walnuts and any other flourishes you'd like to add. For a special occasion, I recommend dark chocolate decorations.

Here's a picture of when I did exactly that:

Happy baking! Let me know if you're making the recipe and how it turned out for you.

If you're gluten free, I do not recommend trying this recipe, as GF recipes need to be specially adapted. However, I do have a GF coffee and walnut cake recipe that I've just started testing and it was brilliant the first time. If you'd like to have a go yourself, do reach out to me on social media and I'll send you the recipe for that!

BOOKS IN THE SERIES

A REVIEW IS WORTH ITS WEIGHT IN GOLD!

I really hope you enjoyed reading this story. I was wondering if you could spare a couple of moments to rate and review this book? As an indie author, one of the best ways you can help support my dream of being an author is to leave me a review on your favourite online book store, or even tell your friends.

Reviews help other readers, just like you, to take a chance on a new writer!

Thank you!
Myrtle Morse

ALSO BY MYRTLE MORSE

BOOKS BY MYRTLE MORSE WRITING AS RUBY LOREN:

THE WITCHES OF WORMWOOD MYSTERIES

Mandrake and a Murder

Vervain and a Victim

Feverfew and False Friends

Aconite and Accusations

Belladonna and a Body

Prequel: Hemlock and Hedge

MADIGAN AMOS ZOO MYSTERIES

Penguins and Mortal Peril

The Silence of the Snakes

Murder is a Monkey's Game

Lions and the Living Dead

The Peacock's Poison

A Memory for Murder

Whales and a Watery Grave

Chameleons and a Corpse

Foxes and Fatal Attraction

Monday's Murderer

Prequel: Parrots and Payback

DIANA FLOWERS FLORICULTURE MYSTERIES

Gardenias and a Grave Mistake

Delphiniums and Deception

Poinsettias and the Perfect Crime

Peonies and Poison

The Lord Beneath the Lupins

Prequel: The Florist and the Funeral

HOLLY WINTER MYSTERIES

Snowed in with Death

A Fatal Frost

Murder Beneath the Mistletoe

Winter's Last Victim

EMILY MANSION OLD HOUSE MYSTERIES

The Lavender of Larch Hall

The Leaves of Llewellyn Keep

The Snow of Severly Castle

The Frost of Friston Manor

The Heart of Heathley House

JANUARY CHEVALIER SUPERNATURAL MYSTERIES

Death's Dark Horse

Death's Hexed Hobnobs

Death's Endless Enchanter

Death's Ethereal Enemy

Death's Last Laugh

Prequel: Death's Reckless Reaper

Printed in Great Britain
by Amazon